MY BESTIES 4
Revenge Is Mine

A Novel

Asia Hill

Good 2 Go Publishing

ISBN: 978-1-943686-61-2

Copyright ©2016 Good2Go Publishing

Published 2016 by Good2Go Publishing

7311 W. Glass Lane • Laveen, AZ 85339

www.good2gopublishing.com

twitter @good2gobooks

G2G@good2gopublishing.com

Facebook.com/good2gopublishing

ThirdLane Marketing: Brian James

Brian@good2gopublishing.com

Cover design: Davida Baldwin

Interior Layout: Mychea, Inc

Printed in the USA

ACKNOWLEDGMENTS

All praises due to Allah. I count my blessings every single day. I am so thankful for the gift that he has given me.

Jae'lyn, Ja'taya, and Jacob. What more can I say? You guys are my life and my world. I am nothing without you.

To the real LockJaw . . . my man, my best friend, my better half, my boo, thank you! I love you so much. Not only do I wanna spend the rest of my life with you, how 'bout eternity? I never knew a real love existed until I met you. I love you forever and some more shit!

A very special thank you to all of my readers. Thank you for liking what I do. That gives me the extra motivation to keep writing these stories. I greatly appreciate the support.

Rachel Hanson (aka Ray Ray) – I didn't know there were still some real people out there until I met you. I love you buddy.

Dominica Glover – Sorry it took me this long to shout you out, cuz . . . you know I love you!

Shalonda (Chicago) Brown, Christine (Pooh) Perkins, Shannon Spivey, and Clarissa Ayo – it was a pleasure knowing you girls. We had a ton of laughs and cries that I wouldn't change for the world . . . I love all of ya'll. The end of my 10-year sentence is near. I have lost so much, but I have also gained a lot. So many tears have been shed. I had to grow up in here. I love the woman that I have become. I will never forget this experience. This is not a place for any civilized human being. Some of these prison officials mistreat you and abuse their authority. They try their best to make every day more miserable than the one before. Remember that!

A shout out to all of the woman and men behind these walls. Be strong. Stay strong. Physically, they have our bodies. Never let them capture your mind.

One Love!

MY BESTIES 4
Revenge Is Mine

PREFACE

There is a dark storm brewing over the City of Chicago. I urge you to take cover . . . immediately. The Eastside Crazy Crew is out for blood!

Revenge is all Ja'ziya has on her mind after being viciously attacked on her way out of jail. After learning the real reason behind her attack, she is going to stop at nothing to make sure Mia gets what she so rightfully deserves. Can she successfully pull off her plan without it blowing up in her face?

Being the enforcer of the crew, Dirty E knows that it's her job to keep her besties safe. It's clean-up time. Anybody who crosses the E.S.C. has to go. Will she succeed in eliminating their problems or will the hunter become the hunted?

RcRe is so fed up with Dirty E protecting JoJo. She is determined to do whatever it takes to kill JoJo, her unborn baby, and her conniving sister, Mia, even if it means destroying her friendship with Dirty E.

LockJaw knows that he is the reason for the attack on Ja'ziya. The only thing on his mind is murder! Can he get revenge for his beloved JuJu, or will he fall victim to Mia's treacherous ways?

The only thing Lil Man wants to do is find JoJo and get his baby. Will his love for his child be the death of him? Guns cocked and loaded, the Eastside Crazy Crew strap up for the last showdown. Enemies better take cover. Can the crew get the revenge that they want or will they bite off more than they can chew?

Getting money is the last thing on their mind. Get ready to find out how they plot and scheme in Revenge Is Mine!

ONE

JuJu

I swear in a million years I never saw that coming. I used to watch all types of prison shows on T.V. and some dude was always getting shanked. I never thought that would be my reality. I'm salty as hell. She got me good . . . 30 stitches in my neck and 15 across my chest. I guess the ass-whooping I put on her was too much. I lost so much blood that by the time they got me to the hospital, I needed to have two blood transfusions. The morphine drip that they had me hooked up to did nothing. I was in so much pain.

"Where the fuck is the nurse's button?"

I pressed it twice and waited. Ten minutes later the nurse entered the room.

"Um, can you please give me something else for the pain? This morphine drip ain't working."

She looked at me with an evil-ass look. Her face was covered with one of those masks that the doctors wear in surgery. There was something familiar about her eyes though. They were cold. I've seen those eyes before. She turned to close the door, still not saying a word. When she turned back around, I almost pissed on myself. She took the mask off.

"So we meet again. I told you that he was going to be mine. You have to die. Simple as that."

"You punk ass bitch. Killing me ain't gon' make him be with you. You was just something to do."

I knew that death was knocking at my door. I just couldn't help myself. If I was about to die, I wasn't about to tuck my tail for this bitch.

"Talk that tough shit all you want, lil' girl. I'm going to have my way with Jaw. I just wanted you to know that."

She pulled out a big-ass needle filled with a light green substance.

"I hope this acid burns you real slowly."

I was too weak to fight her off and the wound in my neck prevented me from screaming out. I couldn't give this bitch the satisfaction of knowing that I was truly scared. I closed my eyes and said a quick prayer. She grabbed my I.V. and pushed the acid into the tube. It almost instantly started to burn. My body started to convulse and jump without my control. I held my breath for as long as I could before I couldn't hold it anymore.

"ARGHHH, FUCK YOU BITCH! I'LL SEE YOU IN HELL"

She stood over me smiling.

"Indeed you will, but before I get there I'ma fuck Jaw until I can't fuck him no more.

Before she walked out, she blew me a kiss. That was definitely the kiss of death.

Lil Mama

My heart was in pieces. I tried to be the best role model I could be under the circumstances. I taught her what I knew. Yeah, she was out there wilding out with her crew, but so fucking what. She didn't deserve this. She had a rough life growing up. Whatever she wanted to do, I was going to make sure she was the best at it. My job was to just . . . I don't know . . . I'm rambling on here trying to convince myself that it's not my fault when in all actuality it was. I was supposed to make sure she stayed in school and got good grades. Instead, I was out here teaching her the same thing that got me 10 years in federal prison. Fuck all that, I'm not about to sit up here and feel sorry for the life that I chose to live. I'm just so happy that the knife didn't hit any major arteries. Whoever did this was going to pay. My phone brought me out of my thoughts.

"Hey boo."

"Hey love, where you at?"

"Up at the hospital with my niece."

"Oh yeah? How is she?"

"Touch and go, but she's going to be okay. Where you at?"

"Still in Indiana. After I make a few moves I'ma shoot your way. You need anything?"

"Just you."

"I'll be there soon."

"Okay, see you soon."

I hung up the phone feeling like a gitty school girl. I recently started talking to someone. I met Carmen at the casino in Hammond, Indiana a few weeks ago. I was at the blackjack table trying to win back the 12 grand that I had just lost. Lately my luck had been on the down side. I had just won a hand when I got a whiff of my favorite men's cologne—Cool Water. What? I'm old school. I turned around to see who had on my shit. Nobody in particular jumped out to me, so I turned back around.

"You looking for me7"

I turned around to see this fine-ass girl standing beside me. I was impressed.

"Maybe I am. Come here. Let me smell your neck."

She leaned over me putting her neck in my face. I took a deep breath. Damn, she smelled good.

"Girl, you smell too good. What's your name?"

"Cee."

"Cee what? We grown. I want your government name."

She smiled and took a seat next to me.

"My bad. My name is Carmen."

"Well nice to meet you. I'm Lil Mama."

She paused for a minute then gave me that 'really' look. We started cracking up at the same time.

"I can't get your government name?"

"Uh uh, I don't know you like that. Where you from?"

"I'm from Gary, Indiana. You?"

"Windy City, baby. What'chu doing at the boat?"

"Damn, girl, you the police? What's good with all the questions?"

"Shit I'm nosey."

We sat at the bar and talked all night. She definitely caught my attention. She was roughly six feet tall, light grey eyes, and with a beautiful caramel complexion. She wore shoulder-length dreads with blonde tips. She wasn't a girlie girl, but she wasn't all the way butch. She was just aggressive. I liked that. I wanted to be the only one wearing makeup.

After a few drinks she completely opened up. That was a no-no in my book. I'm very private, but I let her ass talk away. I found out that she grew up hustling with her brother, who she called, Bubba. Let her tell it. He was the man to see in Gary. He had everything on lock. He got so big that he made her stop hustling and put her through truck-driving school. Everything was all good until he and his girlfriend were both murdered on Thanksgiving night. She had to step up and handle his business. From the looks of things, she was doing quite well for herself. She stood before me rocking a pair of True Religions, a white True Religion shirt, and some black and white Yeezy's. We ended the night with a kiss and we've been kicking it ever since.

Back to the present, I stared at my niece with tears in my eyes. My poor baby. I had to do better for her. She deserved.

Machine's beeping

I jumped up and ran over to her bedside. She started moving her head back and forth like she was trying to get away from something.

"Ju, baby wake up. I'm here."

Not a second after I said that, she jumped up.

"Argghhh, bitch, I'ma kill you!"

"What? Kill who? Baby, calm down."

I knew that once she saw that I was sitting in front of her alive and well, she was going to freak out

"Calm down Ju, I'm here."

She opened her eyes and stared at me for a few seconds. I couldn't read her face. I didn't know what the hell she was thinking. I went to reach out and grab her. She snapped! She started frantically looking around for something.

"Ju, baby, what are you looking for?"

She still didn't address me. She busted out and started screaming.

"NURSE! NURSE! Help me, please!"

This girl was losing her mind.

"No, no, no! I know this damn morphine got me tweaking because you . . ." pointing toward me ". . . are not here."

The nurse came running in the room with a doctor.

"What's wrong?"

Ju went crazy!

"She's dead and I see her. Why is she here and she's dead?"

The nurse looked at me and I asked her if she could give us a minute so I could talk to her. I waited 'til the door was closed until I spoke.

"I know you're shocked. But, baby, calm down before I slap the shit out of you."

She stopped screaming and started crying. It took me a full hour to tell her what really happened to me.

"Auntie, you don't know how hard it was for me being in that jail cell thinking that you were dead."

"It was hard staying out of the way until I was better."

"So, Meech had you the whole time?"

"Yes, he did."

She touched my hand and then my face.

"You look so different. Damn, I'm so glad you are here. I need you."

I was so glad to get that out of the way. Now I needed to know why she just had that little outburst. Boo kinda filled me in on her and Jaw's little issues, but she left a lot out, too. I didn't wanna pry in her business, but I wanted to see if I could make things right.

"Why did you just wake up screaming like that? Don't lie to me either. I'm here for you."

She sat up and started to cry.

"I had a bad dream, auntie. That bitch, Mia, put acid in my I.V."

"Mia? Who is . . .?" she snapped.

"The bitching Jaw was fucking!"

"Well calm down. That bitch ain't here. I am."

"I gotta get out of here. I don't feel safe."

"I'll get the doctors to discharge you; and just so you know, that bitch ain't gon' do shit to you."

TWO

ReRe

This has truly been a crazy-ass year. Where do I begin? If you are just tuning in to the "My Besties" series, you are cheating yourselves. Stop reading right now and go cop one, two, and three. If you don't, you'll never understand. For those who have been rocking with us since book one, much love. Anyway, it's a brand new day and my bestie JuJu just beat that double murder. Well technically it was a mistrial. Same thing if you ask me. I didn't go with Lil Mama or Boo because I had a few things to take care of. I wish I could have seen her face when she saw her auntie.

"Poohman."

I went looking for him to let him know I was about to leave. I found him in the closet talking on the phone. What the fuck was he up to? I decided to eavesdrop.

"Are you serious, bruh? Man, I'm not about to tell Re that shit. I told you not to fuck with that bitch. You better hope Ju make it. Hit me later."

I was stuck. Ju better make it?

"Make it from what?"

I was so spaced out that I didn't even realize that I spoke out loud until Poohman turned around.

"Huh? Damn, shawty, why you sneaking up on me like that? Come here."

"Come here, my ass. What the fuck you and Jaw got going on and why the hell are you in the closet talking on the phone?"

"You know I'm not about to sugar-coat shit with you. Somebody stabbed JuJu when she was getting ready to leave the jail."

My head started spinning. I began seeing those little black spots you see when you get up too fast. Only I wasn't getting up. I was going down. Before I knew it, Poohman was standing over me with a wet towel.

"Damn, Re, yo ass went down like the Titanic. Let me help you up."

He picked me up and walked me over to the bed. After he sat me down, I laid my head on his chest for a few minutes trying to process what the fuck he said.

"Poohman, I don't believe you."

He jumped up and looked at me as if I offended him.

"Re, why would I lie?"

"I'm not talking about you lying. I'm talking about you hiding in the closet on the phone. If I didn't come in there, would you have told me?"

"I don't hide shit from you. It wasn't even like that, though. I was in the closet putting some money up in the stash when he called."

I needed to find my bestie.

"Where they take her?"

"I think Holy Christ."

"CHRIST? Damn she's that messed up?"

I called Lil Mama to see what was going on.

"Hey Re."

"Man, why the fuck . . . ."

"Whoa, lil' girl. Don't make me come fuck you up. I'm under enough stress. I will beat yo ass so bad you'll be laying in the hospital bed next to JuJu."

How could I respond to that? Damn!

"My bad, Lil Mama, I'm just frustrated."

"I understand. Who told you about her being in the hospital?"

"I overheard a conversation that Jaw and Poohman were having."

"Jaw? How did Jaw . . . never mind. She's not at the hospital anymore. She's with me at my house. Let her rest tonight. You can come over tomorrow after you get out of school."

"School?"

"Yes, school. Ya'll little motherfuckers must have lost your way. I'm putting my foot down. I don't know what y'all's problem is, but school is going to become the number one priority. I don't know what to say about y'all. All of you guys had straight A's. Instead of trying to graduate from school, ya'll chose to graduate to a life of crime. Now I fucked up by letting your little crime sprees get out of control. After this shit with my niece, I've had enough."

Okay. I didn't even know she felt like that. Granted, we all had plans, but money was tight. We had to make some moves. But after losing Tiki and Tyesha, I'm now second-guessing our purpose. I do know that I'm going to finish what we started. I have to. It's a must that Jon and Lil Man die. Especially Lil Man! After all that is taken care of, maybe we can go back to being teenagers and doing regular teen stuff. I was tired of the dumb shit. I turned and looked at Poohman.

"After we take care of Lil Man and that bitch JoJo, I'm going back to finish school and maybe go to college. I need to do some positive shit."

He looked at me and smiled. I could tell he was surprised. At least he had my back.

"It ain't like we need money. Go ahead and finish school, boo. I got you."

I sat down and laid back on his chest. He started laughing.

"Wha' you laughing at?"

"Lil Mama scared yo ass straight."

"Shut up."

THREE

Mia

❝I'm going to make Jaw love me if it's the last thing I do. He needs a real woman in his life. He loves me. I know it."

"You love him? Bitch, you slow as hell. That nigga don't want you."

I looked at Lil Man and was about to slap the shit out of him 'til I thought about it first. Little did he know that his days on this earth were definitely numbered. I just had to play my cards right.

"Fuck you punk. You don't know shit. He does love me. We are going to be together. I just have to make sure that JuJu is out of the picture permanently."

"I will say this. You fucked up not killing her. You had the chance to get it done. I know she gon' survive."

"How sure are you, Dr. Lil Man?"

"Because if she would have died, the news would have said so by now. They did pick up the story."

Damn, I didn't think about it like that. Fuck! All right, it was time to put Plan B in motion.

"Lil Man, are you gonna help me?"

"Only if you help me find JoJo. I wanna find her before she has my baby and dip."

YUCK! So fucking gross. I could care less about him, my back-stabbing sister, and the little creature she's carrying.

"I'll help you. What chu gon' do when you find her?"

He lit the cigarette he had behind his ear and blew the smoke in the air.

"Do I really need to tell you? I just want my baby."

"Well she should be due in like six months. That's a little time for me to do my research on Jaw."

"Bitch you's a stalker. That nigga put it on you like that?"

The memories I had in my head of Jaw breaking me off was enough to make me nut all over again. I was about to run my mouth; but when I looked up, that little creep was smiling at me,

"None of your fucking business."

Jaw

"Auntie Boo, I really need to know where she's at. I called the hospital and they said she was discharged."

"I'm up at the jail right now trying to find out what happened. I don't know where she's at. Call Lil Mama. I'ma call you back because mothafuckers up here acting like what happened is top secret. They gon' tell me something or I'ma tear this mothafucker up."

I hung up feeling helpless. I needed to see my baby. That bitch, Mia, was going to die a slow and painful death when I got ahold of her. I felt so fucking stupid. I had to make things right. After calling and talking to Poohman, I felt even worse. That girl was a dead bitch walking.

Ring, Ring

My ringing phone actually scared the shit out of me.

"Who the fuck is this calling me private?"

"Baby, why don't you love me?"

"Mia? What the fuck is wrong with you."

"Jaw, I'm in love with you. I swear I'm the better woman for you."

I needed to play nice with this bitch. Once I got my hands around her neck, I was gonna snap it!

"Man, shawty, you wilding out. Why you get that girl stabbed like that?"

"I didn't mean for her to get hurt. I only wanted to scare her, but fuck her! What about us? Please give us another try. I can make shit right. Please just give me one more chance."

I couldn't believe the pleas this bitch was making. Damn, was the dick that good? I had a plan.

"Man, yo as crazy, but I kinda like that shit."

"Baby I'll do anything for you. You got my word. Baby, can I see you?"

"I don't know. Yo ass on punishment. I'ma hit you in a few hours. You still got the same number?"

"Yeah, boo. Please call me back."

"A'ight."

I hung up and pressed the stop button on the side of my phone. I secretly recorded the phone conversation. I called the one mothafucker that I knew wasn't afraid to body a bitch—

Young Meech.

"Jaw, my dude, what's cracking?"

"Man, Young, I need yo help."

"What's wrong boss?"

"Not over the phone. Where you at?"

"At my spot on 42nd and Princeton."

"Yo spot?"

"Yeah I got a lil' spot on the low end. Me, your brothers, and my partner, Slim 'bout to shut shit down over here. Just call us the Chi City Boys."

"Okay then. Make me know it, Young."

"Come through"

"One."

OUR

Dirty E

"JoJo, you might wanna go in my bedroom."

"Why?"

"Because Re 'bout to come through and holler at me about something. You know it ain't no fucking secret that she fucking hates you."

"I'm not thinking about Re. I live here too."

"Man, kill all that noise and do what I said."

She jumped up and stomped away. All I could do was shake my head. I was dead wrong for having her in my spot knowing the history. ReRe wants to kill this girl and her sister. I couldn't care less about her sister. I kind of care about JoJo. Call me soft, but I don't give a fuck. She's pregnant! I ain't no cold-blooded killer. Well maybe I am, but looking at all the circumstances. She really didn't have a choice being brought into the equation.

Knock, Knock

In walked my bestie looking 10 years older than the last time I saw her.

"Re, what's wrong with you?"

"Sit down, I need to holla at you about JuJu."

"Ju? Where she at? I know she got out the other day."

"Somebody stabbed her up before she could make it up out of the county."

"WHAT?"

I didn't realize what I was doing until I threw my PlayStation controller into the wall.

"Who the fuck did that to her?"

Before Re could answer, JoJo ran into the room.

"E, what's wrong?"

I didn't even get a chance to say shit before Re pulled her gun out and pointed it at JoJo's head. I quickly jumped in the way. I couldn't let my bestie shoot and kill this girl, especially not in my apartment.

"WHOA, RE! NO!"

"NO? Nigga move out of my way before I shoot you too!"

Shit! I was fucked. Why? Because that crazy bitch will shoot me.

"Come on bestie, respect my crib. Put yo gun down."

With my back to JoJo I never saw her pull her gun out until I heard it cock.

Click, Clack

I stood in between them both looking back and forth.

"JoJo, what the fuck? Where'd you get that?"

"I told you, E, anybody that comes for me is going to have to shoot it out. I'm not going. Re, I ain't did shit to you."

"Bitch, fuck you. You are the enemy."

"How, Re? I never did anything to you."

"You was plotting on E and . . . ."

"Bitch, ya'll robbed and killed both of my brothers and my cousin." She started crying but she went on. "If you was in my shoes, you would have done the same thing. Probably worse."

I was shocked. JoJo said that shit with so much conviction and passion that it touched my heart. I played a part in her misery and pain. The look on ReRe's face scared me though. When she's on her murder shit and she's about to kill something, her emerald green eyes sparkle, but not in a good way. It's kind of like a demonic glow. All hell was about to break loose unless I did something fast.

Click, Clack

Re cocked her gun.

"Man ya'll bitches better chill before ya'll accidently shoot me."

JoJo started to put her gun down thinking that Re was about to do the same thing. As soon as JoJo put her gun down

POW!

Re shot.

"RE! WHAT THE FUCK!"

She shot a hole in my wall, missing JoJo's head by at least an inch.

Re looked at me, rolled her eyes, and walked towards the door.

"I missed on purpose. Next time I see you, I'ma put a bullet in your head. E can't save you. You know why? Because I'll shoot her ass, too!"

And just like the she walked out the door.

This shit was getting out of control. All this violence was bad on the economy. I was about to say something to JoJo 'til she raised her hand stopping me.

"E, I'm not going to tolerate that shit. I know that's your best friend and all, but I'm fighting for two lives, not one. The next time she comes for me, one of us is gonna die."

"Just calm down. I'ma talk to her."

"Fuck talking to her. That bitch just shot at me. She not listening to you. I'm gone."

"You not going nowhere. It's not safe out there for you. Let me handle it."

"You better handle it or I'ma handle her."

She walked in my bedroom and slammed my door.

"Don't be slamming my doors. You don't pay rent in here, girl."

FIVE

Young Meech

"I been that nigga. I been that nigga. My dawg's a shooter, so please don't make me send that nigga."

Man that Meek Mill goes so hard. True story though. I'm out here trying to get my kingpin status on. Ever since I hollered at Money Man, and got him and Outlaw on my team, our pockets have been getting fat like fat hoes at a buffet. Not wanting to step on Jaw's toes, we set up shop on the low end. You wouldn't believe how much money there is down here. I even recruited some of the local dudes to be lookouts. If you feed the hood, then the hood will let you eat.

Shit ain't been all good for me though in my personal life. I miss my Auntie Shawn. Damn that nigga Lil Man fucked my world up. I didn't want this for myself. No bullshit! I wanted to follow my homie Slim to college and major in computer engineering.

Yeah, ya boy had dreams. I was my aunt's beneficiary to her estate. She left me a little over $2 million. Her life insurance policy paid me an additional $650,000. Being in the game, you gotta have insurance on your life. You never know what will happen. I needed to have an attorney oversee the finances since I was still a minor. I didn't want him all in my business like that, so I paid him like $100,000 to sign over his rights to Lil Mama. I'm still staying in my aunt's crib. I had some professional cleaners come out and clean the basement from top to bottom. I thought about selling the house; but after all the blood, sweat, and tears my aunt put in this place, I changed my mind. I just got a call from Jaw and homie didn't sound well at all. I was on a money hunt right now. I put my murder game on the back burner for now.

"A Young?"

"Whud up, boy?"

"It's a Blue Charger outside. Want me to go check it out for you?"

"Nah, I got it homie."

When I jumped in the car, Jaw's ass looked stressed out.

"Damn nigga, you look like you in yo 50's. Old looking ass nigga, what's good?"

"It's all bad, Young. I fucked around and cheated on Ju with this lil' hoe I met awhile back. Turns out she was Big Moe's cousin."

"Whoa. You bogus."

"That ain't even the half. Ju ended up finding out."

"I know she took that hard. You slipping."

"Tell me about it, but there's more. The bitch ended up trying to get me killed."

"What type of hoe you dealing with?"

"She tried to get me to kill ME."

HUH? That nigga was tripping.

"Come again?"

"When I met her, I told her my name was L.J. Remember that lil bitch JoJo?"

"Yeah the lil' hoe Lil Man was with."

"Well ol' girl is her older sister. Apparently, JoJo and Mia had a plan to get at me. They were trying to make JuJu mad. JoJo knew me as Jaw and Mia had never met me before. You see where I'm going with this'?"

"Yeah I got you."

"Long story short, Mia had Ju stabbed on her way out of jail."

"Stabbed? Damn I'm sorry to hear that. She good?"

"She fucked up, but she gon' make it. I need to find out where she's at."

"What you want me to do?"

"The girl keeps calling me trying to hook up with me. Bruh, the lil' hoe got problems. Look, listen to this. I recorded our phone conversation."

I was actually in shock when he played the recording for me.

"Man, that girl is crazy."

"I'ma get her to meet up with me then I'ma blow her brains out."

"Don't go by yourself."

"I'm good. I just need you to be my alibi. I think Lil Mama got JuJu put up somewhere. I wanna see her so bad. I just need to handle that crazy girl before she causes any more problems."

"I feel you, but you should tell JuJu."

He looked at me like I had lost my mind.

"Nigga, what? Tell Ju? If I do that, I know I'm a dead man."

"I'm just saying."

We chopped it up for a few more minutes before he readied to leave.

"Jaw, whatever you do, don't go by yourself."

"Man, I'm not worried about that girl."

# Six

Carmen

"Hey niecy pooh, what's good?"

"Can you come take me shopping? I need some new clothes."

"I'ma pick you up on Friday."

"Okay, love you."

"Love you too, Spooky Pooky."

"I hate when you call me that."

"Bye, lil' girl."

I promised myself that I was going to do everything in my power to find out who killed her father . . . my brother. What's good people? I'm Carmen, aka Big Cee. I currently hold the spot as Queen Bitch of Gary, Indiana. My brother, Bubba, was the king nigga in charge. We grew up in poverty. No daddy, dope fiend-ass mother . . . you know the usual. Gary was the murder capital for a long time. You had to be on you're A-game at all times. Bubba and his best friend, King, started hustling at a young age. I hung out with King's sister, Shawn. We went to school together, played together . . . hell, we were practically joined at the hip.

I knew at a young age that I liked girls. Shawn did, too. She was blunt about her shit. I was quiet with my business. Bubba tried to keep the drug game away from me. That all changed the day that King and Bubba's spot was robbed. Shawn saved their lives that day. My brother was still shot in the process. Once he saw that King was schooling Shawn on the ins and outs of the game, he put me up on game, too. Bubba and I grew extremely close. Things between him and King started going wrong. I knew it had something to do with the fact that Bubba was fucking King's baby mama. Word on the streets was that King's baby mama was stealing work from King and giving it to my brother. King ended up getting killed some years back. Bubba told me he was car jacked.

I knew better. After King died, Bubba changed. He got cocky and arrogant. His reckless ways were going to land him in jail if he didn't slow down. I decided to quit hustling for a while and get my CDL. One of us needed a legal job. Shawn stepped up and took over where King left off. My girl was handling her business, too. We stayed in touch and kicked it whenever we had free time.

Thanksgiving changed my life forever. That night I lost my best friend and my brother. Shawn was killed in her own house. My brother's friend told me that four gunmen broke into my brother's Englewood home and gunned him and his girl down. I don't give a fuck how grimy he was, he didn't deserve to die like that. Somebody was going to pay for that shit. Trust me! I got a few people looking into that shit for me. I'm showing no mercy. Just thinking about it makes my heart race. All I do is drink and gamble. My head is all fucked up. Thankfully, I met this fine chocolate thang. Lil Mama got her shit together. I need some type of balance in my life right now. My niece, Spooky, is a lot to handle. She got her father running through her veins. I told her that I was going to find her father's killer. I was about to tear the streets of Chicago up!

Boo

There never was peace around this mothafuckin' city. I'm sick of being here. I been back and forth from my house to the county jail for three days trying to find out who stabbed my godbaby. Today was no different. When I walked in the lobby, the shift lieutenant saw me and put his head down.

"Come on, Ms. Georgetta, not today. I told you we are doing all that we can."

"That shit you talking ain't enough. I'm going to keep coming up to this motherfucka until I'm satisfied."

"We are still on lockdown. I'm taking this matter very serious. Please stop looking at me like that. You are really making me nervous."

Ole punk-ass mothafucker.

"You should be nervous. I'll tell you what, if I don' get my answers soon, all the people that worked the shift that she was stabbed on are gon' be at the unemployment office together!"

I walked out of the county feeling helpless. I needed to get to the bottom of this. You got me fucked up if you think I was going to let this shit slide.

(Ring, Ring)

"Hey, is this Boo?"

"Yes, Jade?"

"Yes, ma'am."

"Don't call me ma'am, lil' girl. I ain't that damn old."

"Sorry. I … um found out who stabbed Ju."

I had to stop walking and take a seat on the steps outside the building. It was cold as hell, but I needed to be still.

"Who baby?"

"When she first got here, she whooped three girls at the same time."

I started cracking up. If she couldn't do shit else, she could fight.

"The girl that actually did the stabbing, her name is Marquisha Brown. She said something about her cousin wanting her to stab Ju."

"Oh yeah? Where she from?"

"I believe she from the Greens. As a matter of fact, she's some kin to the Harris' and the Cole's."

"Thank you, baby. When you coming home?"

"It's gon' be a minute. I'm charged with a body. I'ma fight this shit though."

"Just hold ya head up. I'm 'bout to hit your books. What's your info?"

After getting all of her info, I hopped in my car and went to hit up Western Union. After I sent her a few stacks, I called Lil Mama.

"Whatchu want, hoe?"

"I gotcha hoe! Where you at?"

"At the honeycomb hideout."

"Why you all the way out there?"

"Bitch, I'm chilling. JuJu at my crib resting. You should go check on her."

That hoe thinks she slick. She got somebody out there in Hammond with her.

"I will do just that. Who you got out there? B? Redman?"

"Damn, nu-nu. My boo, Cee."

"I don't know him."

"Sure don't."

"Alrighty then. I'm 'bout to go check on my goddaughter, since you outside being a THOT."

"Yo dog ass mammie."

EVEN

JuJu

I had been out of the hospital for two weeks and still no Jaw. I missed him, but I didn't want him to see me like this. I got my stitches out, but my neck was ugly as shit. The only people that I let come see me were my besties. I noticed some hostility between Re and Dirty. I had seen enough.

"What the fuck wrong with ya'll?"

Dirty pulled on her blunt before she spoke.

"That bitch right there is disrespectful."

I tried not to laugh when she pointed at Re.

"You better get your hand out of my face before I break that mother fucka."

"Bitch please. You don't scare me; and just to let you know, you don't scare JoJo either. Leave that damn girl alone."

At that moment, the room became really quiet. It was so quiet you could have heard a rat piss on cotton. I looked at Re and then back at Dirty. There was a storm brewing in my auntie's living room. Re smiled at Dirty. It was a 'bitch, you lucky you my friend' smile.

"E, you can't save that bald-headed bitch. When I want her, I'ma go get that ass."

I was confused.

"Ya'll, what does JoJo have to do with anything?"

"Tell her E!"

I looked at E and waited for an explanation.

"Okay, let's play catch-up. Lil Man was causing so much havoc around here that I got in touch with the one person that I knew could find him. She started feeding me all type of information on him. She wasn't lying, because everything she said he was going to do he did. She even set him up for me."

"So what happened then?"

"After me and Re shot up JoJo's sister's crib trying to get him, she couldn't go back there."

"So where she at?"

"She's been staying with me."

I didn't know how to respond to that one.

"I mean E, ain't this girl the enemy?"

"Yeah and no. Let's be real for a minute. We've done some fucked up shit. She's connected to our situation because we killed her brothers and her cousin. Not that I'm sorry for it, I'm just stating facts. She may have been plotting on me; but when shit got real, she changed her mind. All that girl wanna do is move away and raise her baby."

"Baby? Who got her pregnant?"

"Lil Man."

"Eeew, she gave that lil' dirty-ass nigga some pussy?"

"Yeah, and now all she trying to is get out of town and raise her baby."

I looked at Re.

"So Re, what's the problem on your end?"

"The bitch gots to go! Point blank and period. She was in cahoots with Lil Man and that's unforgiveable. I don't give a fuck about how she came into the picture."

I could see there was no changing her mind, but I still had to try.

"But Re, she's pregnant."

"With Lil Man's baby. He killed Tiki. I'ma kill that bastard-ass baby."

I could see that E was getting mad.

"Re, we ain't no monsters. Haven't enough people died? After Lil Man killed Tiki, he started a war. Yeah, he gotta go . . . and that bitch, Mia. Let that girl live. We need to get back on our shit. Money ain't no problem. This shit has gone too far. Let's finish school and try to live a somewhat normal life."

"Ain't shit gon' be normal without Tiki."

"Okay, we can get Lil Man and Mia, but after that no more, Re."

I looked at Re.

"I agree. My lil' jail experience was not pleasant. If we keep doing all this killing, we gon' end up in jail forever."

"E, you better keep that hoe as far away from me as you can."

I needed to keep a close eye on that damn girl.

EIGHT

Lil Man

I was going through it big time. That bitch, JoJo, ran off with my baby. I didn't know that I could want something so bad other than bloodshed. I just wanted to get revenge for Pancho. In the process of it all, I lost damn near my whole family. I just want my baby. I wasn't trying to go to jail for killing nobody; but if anybody got in my way while I was on this mission to find that no good-ass bitch, JoJo, I was going to murk they asses. I've been trying to lay low but my pockets are suffering. I was tired of asking that bitch Mia for shit. The bitch think's I'm stupid. I know she's tryin' to play nice with me because she knows I'm a killer. I may be young, but you can't manipulate a manipulator. I'll play her little game until I find JoJo. After I find her, I'ma take my baby and kill that hoe. Me and my cousin KeeKee plan on moving down south with some family. His mother put him out because she said that it was all his fault that Baby Dro and BayBay got killed. I was so deep in, though, that I never heard that girl come in until she was in my face.

"What you thinking about?"

"Finding your sister."

"Oh, well you know Valentine's Day is in a couple of days?"

"And?"

"Me and Jaw are going to spend it together."

I know I'm crazy, but this bitch was truly certified!

"And just how are you going to accomplish that? Ju's out of jail. He ain't thinking about you."

I liked fucking with her. I could tell I hit a nerve. She rolled her eyes and smacked her lips.

"Any fucking way, he's not thinking about that lil' girl. Trust me, I put that good-good on him. I got this."

More like no-no. That goofy ass bitch gon' get herself killed. I hoped so. One less mess that I had to make. I was getting bored sitting in this damn house. I think I had a way to find JoJo.

"Mia, can't I find JoJo through her cell phone?"

"Only if her GPS is on. Go on the computer and check. Type in 'find my phone.'"

It was a longshot but I typed it in. Not even two minutes later, it popped up.

"Damn, that hoe's around the corner from my old house."

"Whose crib she at?"

I zoomed in on the phone's image and my blood began boiling. She had to be with Dirty E. I'ma kill 'em both.

JoJo

I felt good going to my first real doctor's appointment. I wanted to make sure everything was all right. This was going to be a very stressful time for me if I didn't get out of the area, but where would I go? I didn't have no money. I couldn't rent my own apartment. My birthday was in March. I was turning 15, but I was still too young to do anything. Calling my nothing-ass sister was out of the question. There was a program that I could get in when I had three months left. Well, that was in three months. What the fuck was I going to do 'til then? I couldn't stay with E. It was too stressful having to watch my back in my own place. I know she meant well, but that fucking friend of hers was gonna end up dead fucking with me. I was on my way out of the doctor's office when I heard somebody call my name. I was so happy to turn around and see a familiar face.

"Damn, cousin, it's been like forever since I've seen your face. Where you been?"

"Trying to stay alive. What the hell are you doing in Chicago? I thought you were living in Gary."

"I'm back and forth. You know my dad died?"

"Oh my goodness, I didn't know that. I'm so sorry. I loved Uncle T like he was my own father. I'm kind of out here on my own. I lost Boogie, Jr., and Ramone."

"Why are you out here alone?"

"It's a long story, Spooky. I'm just trying to have my baby and get out of Chicago."

"Baby? Who the fuck got you pregnant?"

"This crazy-ass nigga named Lil Man. I'm trying to get away from him."

"Where's Mia?"

"Fuck that snake-ass hoe!"

"Enough said! Well, look, Auntie Cee is coming to get me and take me shopping tomorrow. You can come with us. I'm sure she'll be happy to see you."

After exchanging numbers, I went to the bus stop. I had a big ass family. This could be my chance to move. I could go to Gary with my Auntie Cee. I was ready for a new start.

NINE

Lil Mama

"After you finish cooking, clean up your mess."

"Come on, auntie, I ain't no kid. I know how to clean up."

"Not to get all in your business, but when are you going to call Jaw?"

"Excuse my French, but fuck him. He shouldn't have done me like that."

"But Ju, that boy loves you. I know you might not wanna hear it. He fucked up. Forgive him and move on."

"I'ma think about it."

My phone started ringing.

"We are not finished with this conversation, lil' girl!"

It was Boo.

"What up, sis?"

"I found out why JuJu was stabbed."

"Why?"

"Her lil' friend Jade told me that some hoe name Marquisha Brown did it."

"Well, who the hell is that?"

"The cousin of the bitch that Jaw had cheated with."

"Aw hell naw! Here I was just taking up for him, and he's the reason that my niece almost lost her life?"

"Hey hoe, go easy on my nephew. Trust me, he's under enough stress."

"I'm not in this. Once Ju finds out, she's going to blow her top."

"Don't tell her. Let Jaw do it."

I felt her presence behind me. Sure enough, I turned around to see my nosey-ass niece standing behind me. Shit!

"It's too late for that."

"Damn, she was listening, wasn't she?"

"You know she was. Let me call you back."

"So I got stabbed because of Jaw?"

"I think you should just talk to him."

"Okay."

She walked off. I sat there and thought about the whole situation. Damn, shit was about to get real bad for him. I just prayed that Ju didn't do shit to him. I would hate to have to fall out with Boo over this shit.

(Front door slams)

"Ju?"

I looked out of the front window to see my niece jumping in her car and peeling off. Shit! I ran to grab my phone to call Jaw.

Jaw

I needed to see my girl. She wasn't answering my calls and she ain't even bothered to come home yet. Valentine's Day was in days. I just wanted to make things right.

(Ring Ring)

I checked the caller I.D. before I answered it – it was Lil Mama. What the fuck did she want?

"Yo, Lil Mama, what up?"

"Where you at?"

"At the crib. Why?"

"Um, you might wanna get up out of there."

"Why?"

When she told me that Ju knew that Mia was behind her stabbing, I was fucked!

"Fuck! Man I'ma – What the fuck?"

I ran to the window just as she busted out my windshield. She had already got my driver's side window.

"What's wrong?"

"Yo fucking niece is outside busting my car windows. Aye, Ju, you better quit. Girl, I'm not playing."

"Don't open that door. I'm on my way!"

I threw on my Timbs and rat down the stairs two at a time.

"Ja'ziya, what the fuck is wrong with you? Quit doing that to my car."

"Fuck you and this car. You had that bitch in this car didn't you?"

I knew better than to answer that.

"Come inside, baby. It's cold. Let's go talk about it. Come on, the police are probably on the way."

"Fuck the police. I got stabbed because you couldn't keep your dick in your pants. You's a stupid mothafucker. All you had to do was leave me alone."

That shit ate me alive. She had tears and snot running down her face. Damn, I felt like shit.

"Look at my fucking neck!"

She pulled her scarf off and I almost cried. That bitch fucked up my baby's neck. I walked closer to her and held my arms out.

"Come on, baby, let me talk to you."

She dropped the bat and walked past me, heading for the house.

"You lucky I'm cold?"

I didn't want her to know that I was desperate. I needed her to forgive me. When I made it upstairs, she had her suitcase out packing her shit.

"You ain't shit. I would have never did you like that. I hope her pussy was worth it."

"Man, Ju, I know I fucked up. I'm admitting that. I was wrong. But on my momma, you might as well quit packing. You not going nowhere."

After I snatched her suitcase away from her, I grabbed her. She seemed to calm down some.

"I know I hurt you. Let me make it right."

I saw the look of exhaustion on her face, so I took full advantage of the situation. I took off her coat and sat her down on the bed. I took off her boots and sat next to her. She didn't say anything. All she did was cry. That broke my heart.

"Let me make it up to you."

"How are you going to do that? You broke my heart."

"I have no excuse for what I did, but I'm not letting what she did to you slide. Please just let me handle this."

"I told her all about my plan, and with a few kisses, I got her to agree to it.

"Let me call Lil Mama and tell her you good."

"Hello, Jaw? You still alive?"

"Alright now, y'all behave."

I held her all night in my arms. The plan was set in motion. Valentine's Day was going to be the last day that bitch, Mia, walked the face of this earth.

TEN

Carmen

"Niecy pooh, where you at?"

"Over here at Money Man's crib."

"You ready to go shopping?"

"Yeah, auntie. Guess who I ran into?"

"Who?"

"JoJo."

"Are you serious? Where'd you see her at?"

"It's a long story. I'll tell you when you get here. Can she go with us?"

"Yeah. I'm on my way."

My damn niece was so spoiled. I didn't mind though. I hadn't seen JoJo since she was five years old. Her mother's boyfriend threw her off of the project building, killing her. Her grandma was left to pick up the slack. Mia could have done a better job. I wondered why she failed to mention that JoJo was even over this way. She cops from me once a month. I'ma fuck Mia's ass up. Family comes first.

Two hours later

I was almost in tears as I looked at my very pregnant niece, JoJo. My poor baby. I wish I would have stepped in a long time ago. I told her to tell me the whole story and no matter what, don't lie. After she got finished, I was furious. I had no idea that Boogie, Jr. and Ramone had even died. Mia's ass was foul.

"Auntie Cee, I just wanna finish school and raise my baby. Mia has lost her mind. Please don't even tell her that you saw me. She is on a mission to self-destruction."

"Let me handle Mia. You wanna come to Gary and stay with me?"

"Can I think about it? I got a few things that I need to get in order."

"Hurry up. I don't want you out here in these streets."

"I got Spooky's crazy butt on speed dial. I'm good."

After taking my nieces shopping, I dropped them off because I had moves to make. I was definitely gonna handle Mia's ass the next time she came to cop something from me. What type of sister was she?

Ring Ring

"Hey sexy, you ready for me?"

"Yes I am. Where you at, boo?"

"I just dropped my nieces off. Where you at?"

"Home."

"Yo niece still there?"

"Naw, she at her boyfriend's?"

"I'm on my way."

"You know it's Valentine's Day tomorrow?"

"I know. I got you something."

Mia

I had a small bag packed. I was ready for my date with my man. I got this wild night planned to the tee. First, we're going to have an enjoyable dinner overlooking the city's skyline. After that, we got a nice suite at the Hyatt downtown. I made it my business to rent the presidential suite on the top floor. I was hoping we can end the night by fucking 'til the sun rises. Let me call him and see where he is. I was ready to get shit popping.

"What up?"

"Hey baby, where are we meeting at?"

"I was trying to come chill at your crib for a minute."

Should I let him know where I stay? I could knock him out and tie his ass up in the basement and keep him there forever. That was starting to sound like a better plan.

"We could do that. Just pick me up some Patron."

"What's yo address?"

"4231 South Princeton."

"I'm on my way."

Change of plans. I ran downstairs to my basement and made a few adjustments to my special room. I had a room dedicated to Jaw. His pictures were all over my walls. I had this big-ass, queen-size bed that I would lay on and masturbate while looking at his pictures. I was so busy fixing things that I never heard Lil Man creep up on me.

"Damn, what the fuck we got down here?"

"It's my new love nest for me and Jaw. He 'bout to come over here."

"You should kidnap his ass and keep him here."

"Will you help me?"

"Bitch, yo ass is crazy for real. You better hope you don't end up dead down here. How the hell you get all these pictures of him anyway? Let me find out you really been stalking that nigga."

"I just keep tabs on him, that's all."

"Okay, well, if I help you get him in here, you gotta let me see your car."

"Help me and I'll think about it."

I called Jaw back.

"Hey, I gotta make a move. Meet me on 55th at that Checkers."

"Mia ain't no Checkers there no more."

"You know where I'm talking about though."

"Yeah, I'll be there."

"A'ight baby."

ELEVEN

Young Meech

❝❝Hey, turn the music down. My phone ringing."

It was Jaw.

"Whud up, playboy?"

"Young, I'm 'bout to meet up with that hoe, Mia."

"Man, you want me to come follow you?"

I'm 'posed to meet her on 55th and the Dan Ryan. Come where the old Checkers used to be."

"A'ight. Me and my boy, Slim, 'bout to ride up there. Yo brothers at the spot in Englewood."

(20 minutes later)

I pulled up behind Jaw and parked. My boy, Slim, and me jumped out and greeted my boy. When Jaw stepped out of the car, he started mugging instantly. I was stuck.

"Ya'll know each other? Jaw you good?"

"You know this nigga?"

"Yeah, we grew up together."

I was looking back and forth from Slim to Jaw. I was waiting on somebody to give me an explanation. I looked back at Slim. He had a big-ass smirk on his face.

"Slim, say something."

"Dude's mugging me because me and his girl know each other. He came up to the county one day when I was visiting her."

Well I'll be damned! This was a small world. Jaw looked like he was about to POP!

"You ain't talking all that shit now nigga."

Slim laughed.

"Nigga, I wasn't talking shit then. I told you to ask your girl. You mugging for no reason."

"Whatever lil' nigga. Young you good. You ain't gotta wait on me, I'm good."

"This shit ain't even that serious, Jaw. I'm here for you, nigga."

"Well I'm telling you I'm good."

And just like that he jumped in his car and pulled off. Slim started cracking up.

"Slim, that shit ain't funny."

"Fuck that sensitive-ass nigga. Me and shawty cool. I ain't got shit to do with what he got going on. Shit, he shouldn't have cheated."

"Who told you he cheated?"

"His girl."

"Let's ride."

I thought about the situation, and it didn't sit well with me. I grabbed my phone and hit Boo's line.

"Hello?"

"Hey Boo . . . this Meech."

"Hey baby. How are you?"

"I'm good. Look Jaw, tryna meet that crazy-ass girl Mia by his self."

"By his self?"

"I met up with him and he got pissed because I had my boy with me. Apparently, my boy knows Ju. Jaw ran into him at the county when he was visiting her."

"Damn. Okay, I'll look into it."

"Thank you."

Boo

Yo, leave a message."

"This yo auntie. Call me back now. I know you ain't in your chest about that lil' boy."

I hung up and called back three more times, only to get the same results . . . nothing!

Something ain't right. Mad or not, he will answer his phone for me. Shit, now I gotta call Heidi.

"Hey hoe. Happy Valentine's Day. What chu doing?"

"Trying to figure out where your son is."

"My son? Jaw?"

"He was on his way to meet that crazy-ass girl, Mia."

"By his self?"

"Yeah."

"Come get me right now, damn it!"

20 minutes later

I pulled up to her crib and blew the horn. As serious as the situation was, I almost died from laughter when that damn Heidi came outside. She was cute, but this was not the time to be wearing that shit. She looked like Jessica Rabbit in a tight-ass red dress with 5-inch stilettos and a white fur coat. She came strutting to my car like she just got off of the runway on her way to a pimps-up, hoes-down party. I didn't even bother to unlock my door for her ass. I cracked the window.

"Bitch, quit playing and unlock the door. It's cold."

"Take yo ass back in the house and change. You know better."

"So I'm not going to be able to make it to my dinner date? Damn it, Boo! I knew I shouldn't have answered the phone. What a waste of a nice dress. You ain't shit."

She stormed off back to her building and almost slipped on a patch of black ice. I started cracking up, and I honked my horn lettering her know that I saw her.

"Fuck you, Boo!"

TWELVE

Jaw

I felt betrayed. Even though I knew that it wasn't on purpose, I was still mad at Young. That Lil nigga made me feel like shit. It was my own guilt that had me all fucked up, but damn I wanted to hit that lil' boy. I wondered if JuJu had been in touch with him.

Ring Ring

"Yo?"

"Baby, where are you?"

"Come to the gas station on Kings Drive. Who you with?"

"My cousin. She's going to take my car and I'ma ride with you. Is that cool?"

"Yeah, you can drive my car when you get here."

"I love you, baby."

I had to look at the phone for a second. Was this bitch serious? Come on Jaw, take one for the team.

"I love you too."

Click

I didn't think I had that in me. I needed to hurry up and kill this bitch so that I could get back to my girl. She was still at the crib so I was thankful for that. I saw that my Auntie Boo was calling me. I sent her to the voicemail. I wasn't in the mood to talk about shit. I was in the mood to kill.

Mia

"All you have to do is hold this cloth over his face."

"Lil Man, this ain't gon' hurt him is it? I don't want to kill him."

"Na, it's going to knock him the fuck out. After I help you, I'm in the wind."

"Alright."

I dropped Lil Man off at the corner so Jaw wouldn't see him. When I pulled up to the gas station, he was pumping gas. Damn, he looked so fucking sexy. I walked up behind him and put my arms around his waist.

"Did you miss me?"

"Yeah, drive."

Okay then. As soon as he got into the passenger seat and closed the door, I smiled at him. I opened the back door and put my purse on the seat. When he laid his head back on the seat, I made my move. I forced the cloth onto his nose and mouth. In 10 seconds, he was out. I hopped in the driver's seat and pulled off. I called Lil Man.

"Meet me at the house and hurry up. I don't know how long he's gonna be out."

"I'm right behind you."

Once we got to my crib we needed to move fast.

"Lil Man, go get the door."

When he came back, we dragged him in the house and down to the basement. After he was safely secured, I left him alone in the room. It was time to get rid of Lil Man.

"Mia, I'ma take his car."

"Good. Bye."

"Damn . . . lil' thirsty, you ready, huh?"

"Get the fuck out and stay out tonight."

After Lil Man left, I went upstairs and took a hot bath. I took my time getting ready for my man. It wasn't like he was going anywhere no time soon. I hope I did a good job covering my tracks. I didn't need anybody coming after me. I was ready for whatever though. I didn't have to worry about Lil Man's ass saying shit, so I was all good. Tonight was going to be the best night of his life!

Lil Man

"Man, KeeKee, you need to meet me so we can ride around

and look for JoJo."

"Who shit you in?"

"Mine nigga. I hit a lick."

"I'ma hit you when I make it that way. I'm trying to handle some shit right now."

"A'ight. Hit me when you get this way."

I decided to hit a few blocks and get my mind right. For some reason, I couldn't help but wonder if JoJo was over there on Marquette. Her phone showed up in that area, so it was a possibility. I had a feeling that she was over there with that nigga, Dirty E. I'ma kill that bitch. I decided not to wait for KeeKee. I did a quick drive-through just to see if she or one of them bitches were there. I had the upper hand on their asses today. I'm in Jaw's car. They'll never see me coming.

ReRe

"Let me see, Ju. It ain't that bad."

"It's bad enough. I hope the scar fades away. Damn, where the fuck is Jaw? This is the shit I be talking about."

"Where did he say he was going?"

"He said he was going to handle that Mia situation. I don't know, Re. I'm not trusting that shit."

I picked up Ju's phone and called Jaws' phone.

"Re, what you doing?"

"Calling Jaw. It's going straight to the voicemail. I'm about to call Poohman. I'm sure he knows something."

I dialed Poohman's number.

"What's wrong, Ju?"

"Baby, this me. Have you heard from Jaw?"

"Earlier. He said he was able to go handle something, why?"

"Something ain't right. He supposed to be back by now."

"Let me call you back, bay."

I hoped everything went well. I don't think my bestie could talk some more bullshit right now.

"Come on, Ju." We 'bout to hit some corners and scoop up E."

"Okay, I wanna see her anyway."

We called E and she told us to come through. I told her to come outside because I wasn't coming back in her crib. She called me petty and hung up the phone. We parked in front of E's crib. I flamed up a blunt, as E came running out the crib to my car.

"Blast the heat, hoe! I'm cold."

"Where the hell ya coat at, dummy? You know Chicago's winters are brutal!"

E grabbed Ju and hugged her tight. This was her first time seeing Ju outside the house.

"Hey, Elizabeth. I've missed you, too."

"Damn, Ja'ziya, we doing government names now?"

"Jaw's ass ain't answering the phone, E."

E turned her face up at us.

"Jaw just drove past like three minutes before ya'll pulled up."

She turned around to look out the back window.

"There go Jaw right there coming up the street."

True enough, Jaw was driving up the street slow as hell . . . as if he was creeping up on somebody.

"Ju, roll the window down and flag him down."

Let me tell you . . . when Jaw's car stopped on the side of us, we were not ready for what the hell we saw.

"Ju, what the fu . . . ."

"YEAH, BITCHES, SURPRISE!"

THIRTEEN

Money Man

"Call Outlaw."

"I did. He not answering."

Fuck! Where the hell was that nigga? Even though we got a spot with Young Meech on the low end, I wasn't about to give up my spot over here in Englewood. The money over here was crazy. Outlaw has been going back and forth from here to the low-end all weekend. Lil' bro bought his paper. Me and my girl, Spooky, been trapping hard. I gotta admit I was starting to fall for her young ass. I got me at true trap queen. I didn't think that we would ever hit it off like we did. I was on Facebook promoting my new music and shorty emailed me telling me that I was raw with it and she liked my shit. So we hit it off. She was all the way in Gary, Indiana, so I thought that it was going to be on some long-distance type shit. I thought wrong! Shorty showed up at my OG's crib with her suitcase and a wad of hundreds.

She was even bold enough to ask my OG if she could co-sign for an apartment for us.

Heidi looked at her and said, "Hell naw, you not about to fuck up my credibility. You can pay me rent and stay here." She been with me ever since.

Off the bat I could tell that something was off about her. She told me that she had recently lost her father. I'm usually not with all the sensitive shit; but like I said, I like her. Plus, she had the hookup on some bomb-ass work. She said her auntie is the Queen B in Gary. I didn't care who she was. As long as she kept giving us a good deal on the work, she could be God! Speaking of the devil, my girl came strutting in the spot looking like a super model.

"Damn, boo, you look good. Where you cop that fit from?"

"My auntie took me and my cousin JoJo shopping. I told her that we had a spot over here. She told me that my daddy used to run this side of town."

"Oh yeah? Who was yo daddy?"

"He had a few different names, but everybody mostly called him Big T."

"I never heard of him. Young might know him."

"Oh, I'ma ask him. You hungry?"

"Yeah. What are you 'bout to cook?"

"Cook? Na, playa, I'm 'bout to order some Chinese food."

"Lazy ass!"

Young Meech

"Hey, Lil Mama, when you find the time can you help me pack up all of my Auntie's things?"

"Yes. How about we do it this weekend? I'm drunk in love right now. You know how it go."

"Yeah, I do. When can I meet your boo?"

"Soon, call you later. My boo wants me. Love you son."

Son? That shit just touched me in a major way. Lil Mama and I got a bond that's Ford tough right now. She assumed the role of my mother figure. I saved her life, and to be honest, she saved mine. The night that I lost my sister and my auntie, I wanted to die with them. I even contemplated suicide. I had no one, or so I thought. She was there. So naturally when I saw her wreck her car, I did what I knew she would have done for me. I still hadn't heard from Jaw. Damn my big homie was in his feelings big time about Slim. I had to fix that. Jaw was my nigga.

I called his phone.

Nothing! I called back and left a message.

"Man, Jaw we better than this. Pick up the fucking phone and call me back."

I had a bad feeling in the pit of my stomach. I couldn't shake the feeling that something was wrong. I was about to pick up the phone and call Boo, but my phone rang. It was JuJu.

"What's good?"

"MEECH, LIL MAN GOT JAW'S CAR!"

"WHAT? Where you at?"

She was hysterical. I could barely understand what she was saying.

"Calm down and start from the top, ma. I can't understand you when you screaming."

"Jaw was supposed to meet up with Mia. He wasn't answering the phone. Me and Re went to chill with E at her crib. We were sitting outside smoking when Dirty saw Jaw's car driving up the street. I stuck my hand out the window and waved so he would stop. When the car stopped on the side of us, it wasn't Jaw. It was Lil Man."

"Fuck, I knew I should have went with him."

"What?"

"He called me and told me what he was on and to meet him."

"Why didn't you go?"

"I did; but when I pulled up, I had my boy, Slim with me. For same reason, Jaw got all in his feelings about that."

"You know Slim? OMG!"

"Yeah, we grew up together. How you know him?"

"He went to South Shore. We used to chat on the book. But anyway, what happened?'

"Jaw and Slim had words and Jaw said he was cool. Then he dipped."

"Lil Man screamed 'yeah bitches, surprise' and pulled off. We were all too stuck to do anything. Even if we tried to chase him, it wasn't no way we were gonna catch that car."

"Okay, now it's all starting to make sense. I'm sure that Mia and Lil Man set him up. Ju, that bitch was really obsessed with him. He recorded their phone conversations and played 'em for me. I know she did something to him. I told him not to sleep on that hoe. DAMN!"

The line was quiet for a few seconds. All I could hear was Ju crying.

"Stop that fucking crying. That nigga a'ight. We gon' find him. Round up the crew and meet me at my crib."

"Okay."

FOURTEEN

Jaw

When I came to, I had no idea where the fuck I was. My nose burned like I snorted some bad coke. My vision was blurry. I had to keep opening and closing my eyes trying to adjust. The room was red. When I was able to see clearly, I almost died! I was cuffed to a big-ass bed with a satin red headboard. The sheets and comforter were red and white. At that moment, I knew that Mia wasn't just crazy, that hoe was sick. My pictures covered all the walls. She had a bunch of pictures of me that I don't even remember taking. Then it hit me. That hoe was following me for a minute too. Damn why didn't I let Young come with me? I heard some footsteps coming towards the room. I hoped and prayed that I wasn't that bitch. The locks on the door clicked and the door flew open.

"I see somebody finally woke up. Hey daddy."

"Bitch, I ain't yo fucking daddy. You crazy!"

"No, you are not my daddy, but you will be a daddy before you know it."

"Man, Joe, untie me."

"Hell naw. I'm not that stupid. You have to earn your freedom. Don't you like our little setup? It's quite romantic ain't it?"

"Fuck you."

"Oh, I plan to. This is going to be the best Valentine's Day ever!"

She grabbed my shoes and snatched them off. She then proceeded to crawl on the bed and unbuckled my belt. I saw where this was going.

"Bitch . . . I mean, baby, if we gon' make love, untie me."

"Naw, you good. I just want you to lay here and let me put this pussy on you real slow. I'm going to make you love me."

I couldn't believe that this bitch was about to rape me. This shit wrong. I'm not consenting to this shit. I tried to think of everything that would keep my dick soft. That didn't work. My dick betrayed me. She snatched my pants and my boxers off at the same time. Her eyes lit up when she saw that my dick was rock hard.

"I see somebody missed me."

Before I could respond, she had all nine inches in her mouth. I tried my best not to make a sound. I didn't want her to know that her warm mouth . . . aww shit was the fucking truth. Without my control, my hips started rotating around and around. That gave her the ammunition to go further. She stopped and jumped off of the bed. I was about to ask her why the fuck she stopped, but I wasn't supposed to be enjoying this shit. She went to the nightstand and pulled out this fuckin' toy. I know that ain't what the fuck I think it is! As if reading my mind, she looked at me and smiled.

"Oh relax, it's just a vibrator. Don't worry I'm not going to stick it anywhere you don't want it to go, unless…"

"Bitch, don't play with me. Untie me."

"Nope!"

She climbed back in the bed. She started tongue-kissing my dick. Damn, I hated this bitch, but she was a beast on the head side. She got my dick back hard within seconds. There go my damn hips again. I opened my legs so she could deep-throat all of it. When I did that, she turned on the vibrator and placed it under my balls. They say men got a G-spot, but they never let the girl get close to it because it's too close to their assholes. She put that mothafucker right on my G-spot. That did it. I couldn't hold my moans in any longer.

"Aw, shit, girl, suck that shit. Gah damn, you better suck it, bitch. I hate you. Don't fucking stop."

The instant I said that, she climbed on top of me and slid her panties to the side. Now that's the shit I wasn't with.

"Hell, naw, if you gon' take my shit, put on a rubber, man."

"Didn't I tell you that you was going to be a daddy."

Man, this crazy-ass bitch was trying to make me nut up in her.

"Don't!" was all I got out of my mouth before she slipped my dick into her warm tight pussy. She got on her tippy toes and rocked back and forth slowly on my dick.

"Aww, fuck, Mia . . . bitch. Y-y-y-ou ain't shit. Damn baby, I mean bitch, stop!"

"You might as well shut up and nut. I'ma fuck you like this every day until I get pregnant."

I couldn't say shit. My dick turned against me. I felt the nut building up from the pit of my stomach. I couldn't hold it. I tried to stiff the moan that escaped my lips.

"FUCK!" was all I could say. This dirty-ass bitch sat all the way down on my dick and rotated her hips in a circle.

If I got the chance, I was going to break her fucking neck. There was no way in hell I was letting her have that baby.

FIFTEEN

JuJu

I couldn't believe the change of events. I went from hating Jaw's guts for the pain he caused me to missing the fuck out of him. I was so worried. I didn't know what to do. We all met up at Young's crib to discuss our next move. When I looked at Money Man and Outlaw, I cried. They looked just like their brother. Young did his best to console me. Poohman had a blank expression on his face. Boo was pacing back and forth, and Heidi was smoking squares back to back.

"Heidi, I didn't know you smoked."

"She don't!"

Boo snatched the cigarette out of her hand. I almost laughed.

"Meech, do you think that she will kill him?"

"From what I heard on the recording, no. She got it bad for him ya'll."

"Well, we need to find his car."

"Ju, you are so right, but how?"

"I don't know Outlaw … WAIT!"

I turned to look at Boo and asked, "Do you think Ashley will help us?"

Boo shook her head.

"I don't know. I mean we did save her life, and played a big part in Malone's ass going to jail for life. You know she's a sergeant now?"

"Boo, I think we should call her. We need to have her put a BOL out for his car."

It was a long shot, but I wondered if JoJo knew how to get in touch with her sister. I was desperate.

"E, can you see if JoJo knows where to find Mia?"

The minute I said that, Re's crazy ass rolled her eyes at me and shook her head. I didn't give two fucks. Honestly, she was starting to get on my damn nerves with her bullshit.

"What, Re? What the fuck is your problem?"

"Why trust her word? You think she's going to really give up her sister? Hell no. I don't trust her."

It was my turn to roll my eyes at her ass . . . "Anyway, E?"

"She'll help if she knows something. I'll holler at her tonight."

That was good enough for me. I got up and grabbed the phone off the charger.

"I'm about to call Ashley."

Ashley

Now let me tell you, that was some tantalizing shit I went through. That fat-ass Malone did some fucked up shit to me. Luckily for me, my girl's family found me and ultimately played a big role in getting him put away for life. I have been trying to pick up the pieces of my life. I got promoted to sergeant, and recently I met someone. She's a little different from what I'm used to, but was truly sexy. I even softened up my look to fit hers.

I met her while I was in Indiana getting some gas. You see, gas is so much cheaper in Indiana. Anyway, I pulled up to the pump and got out. It was cold as hell, so I was trying to make my way in the store to pay for my gas. On the way to the counter, I grabbed a Red Bull and a pack of gum.

"Let me get 40 on pump three."

"Let me getcha number!"

I turned around about ready to snap on whoever was all up in my eat. My words got caught in my throat. Damn, she was fine. She even had on my favorite cologne — Cool Water. She had this smooth baby face. Her dreads were on pint . . . just how I like them. To top it all off, she had a pair of light grey eyes. I was stuck.

"Damn, sexy. You gon' tell me your name?"

I could feel my face get all red. I was embarrassed.

"My bad. I'm Ashley. Yours?"

"Carmen, but you can call me Cee."

And just like that, we quickly sparked something special. She visits me every weekend. Her job keeps her busy all week. Fine by me, because I'm off on the weekends.

Back to the present, I was sitting at my desk trying to finish up a case I was working on when my phone rang. I was kind of shocked to see the number.

"Ms. Ja'ziya, how are you?"

"Hey Ash. I'm doing better. I'ma get straight to the point. Jaw is missing."

"Missing? Baby, what's going on?"

"Long story short, he was trying to clean up a mess he made. I guess the girl got the upper hand on him. Lil Man must have helped her, because I saw him driving Jaw's car."

"Lil Man got his car? Oh no, that can't be good. Listen, given me his tag number. I'll put out a BOL on his car."

I hung up and put out that BOL . . . I hoped to God that he wasn't dead.

IXTEEN

Carmen

"No, you need to do what the fuck I'm saying. I said get your ass over here now!"

"What is your problem?"

"I talked to your sister. How could you do her like that?"

"Her? Did she tell you that she's been siding with the enemy?"

"I know everything. What the fuck is wrong with you? Yo ass done fell off. How you go from moving 10 bricks a week to nothing? That nigga got you like that?"

She was quiet for a few minutes.

"I love him, Auntie. We gon' be together."

"Yo ass still crazy? I heard that boy ain't thinking about you."

"Oh yeah? Then why is he here with me right now?"

"Knowing yo ass, he probably there against his own will. Get yo ass over here."

That damn niece of mine has some serious issues. On the hustling side, the girl is a monster. She can move weight better than some of the niggas I know. She just don't need to be in no relationships. Last boy that shitted on her, she killed. It took Bubba and a few hundred thousand to make that shit go away. Speaking of someone that don't need to be in no relationships, I think I bit off more than I can chew. Juggling two women is harder than I thought.

I got Lil Mama who is rough . . . a straight gangsta. I swear I don't have to tell her nothing. She just knows what to do. Then you got my new flavor of the month, Ashley. She's a good girl — sweet, quiet, and willing to please. Nasty as hell in the bedroom. The only reason why she might have the upper hand on Lil Mama is because she's a cop. I might need her first. For now I'ma keep fucking them both. It ain't like I'ma get caught up. Chicago is a big-ass city.

(Ding, Dong)

"Come in."

In walked my niece, Mia. I had to get to the bottom of this shit with her and JoJo. Family sticks together no matter what.

"Sit the fuck down."

Lil Mama

Every time we try and settle these kids down to make them do right, something else happens. I swear these lil' mothafuckers were going to give me gray hairs. I needed my boo to come over here and make everything better. I had been spending so much time with these kids and their bullshit, that I've been neglecting my boo, Cee. Call me paranoid, but I think she been on a little funny business of her own. When she came to see me Sunday night, I could have sworn that I smelled another woman's perfume on her. I think it was Gucci Guilty. Let me find out she on to the next one, I'ma beat her ass. I'ma play it cool until she slip up. This ain't what she want. She better not be cheating on me.

Ring, Ring

"Hello?"

"Whud up ma?"

"Hey, Meech. What's going on?"

"You know I gotchu. How are you and your little crew coming along?"

"Better than I thought. I been putting my money up, too. I don't want to do this shit forever. Can I ask you a question?"

"Shoot."

"Can I call you Mom from now on?"

Damn, I wasn't expecting that. It took everything in me not to break down and cry. This kid has been through hell and back; but through all the bullshit and violence, all he wanted from me was to be my son.

"Of course you can, Meech. Now, after we handle all this business, you have to go back and finish school. I don't want my son to be a damn loser."

"A'ight ma. I gotchu. Love you."

"I love you more, son."

JoJo

Damn, my sister done went too far. Kidnapping? I can't believe she was even able to pull that shit off. I know she had help.

Ring, Ring

I saw a number that I didn't recognize. "Hello?"

"Is this JoJo?"

"Who is this?"

"This is JuJu. Look, I need your help."

"How can I help you?"

"I need to know where your sister is. I think she had something to do with Jaw coming up missing."

"I'm sure she did, but how can I help you? We don't talk."

"Do you know where she might be?"

"She could be anywhere; and if she had help, it was Lil Man."

"I know you ain't lying because Lil Man was driving his car. You might wanna watch your back as well. When is the baby due?"

Damn did everybody know that I was carrying that bastard's baby?

"It's okay JoJo. I'm not out to hurt you or your baby."

"Re is though. I'm due in July. But with all the stress I'm under, I might have her early."

"It's a girl?"

"Yeah, I found out last week. I'm just trying to figure out my next move. I wanna finish school and raise my baby. All this shit is a bit much. I had my reasons for wanting to beef with ya'll, but now JuJu, I just wanna be done with all the foolishness."

"I feel you. That jail shit opened my eyes to a lot of shit. I'm not trying to do no life sentence for murder. I will say this though, if I don't find my man alive, I'm not going to stop until I dismember your sister."

"I'll help you in any way that I can. Just keep Re away from me. She shot at my head the other day. I really don't want no beef."

"I'll do what I can. Be safe and call me if you find out anything."

SEVENTEEN

Money Man

I can't believe that my big brother got kidnapped. The streets ain't safe at all. I'm still tryin' figure out how that hoe pulled that shit off. The show must go on though. Today I was at the spot on 4th and Princeton making it do what it do. Poohman was in Englewood, so we had all angles covered.

"Outlaw, go get the door."

I was trying to finish bagging up before Spooky came over. She had been spending a lot of time with her cousin. I was kinda glad that she had something else to do other than sit up under me in the trap. I was just about done bagging up when I heard Outlaw going off.

"Nigga, you gon' tell me where you got it from or yo' ass gon' die."

I jumped up so fast that I dropped the mirror I was bagging up on. I had to get to him before he shot whoever he was snapping on. When I hit the corner, I paused. Lil' bro had this old-ass crackhead named Freddie on his knees with the banger pointed to his head. This was the last thing we needed. We just opened up shop. It was too early to begin killing people.

"Outlaw, man. Joe, put the gun down. Let me handle it."

"Ain't shit to handle. If he don't tell me what I wanna hear, I'ma POP his punk ass! Look."

He tossed me something in the air. When I caught it, I almost cried when I figured out what it was. It was a platinum chain with an iced-out charm. The charm had the initials L.J. on it. In a blind rage, I pulled out my gun and cocked it.

CLICK, CLACK

"Yo, my man. Where you get this chain from?"

"Ah-h-h, I got it from this chick that lives on my block. She stopped me and asked me if I wanted it."

"What she look like?"

"Cute, light skin, micro braids. Shit, I don't know. I saw the chain and got happy as hell because I knew that I could get my dope with it."

"Where you see her at?"

"Over down on 42nd and Princeton. She was coming out of this red and white crib. I can show you, just don't kill me."

"Let's go!"

Boo

"Hello?"

"Hey Boo, this Ashley."

"Hey girl, what you got?"

"I got a hit on Jaw's car. It was spotted on Marquette."

"That's by Lil Mama and E's crib, ain't it?"

"Yep, there's a patrol car waiting over there for you."

I hung up and called Heidi.

"What now?"

"They found Jaw's car. I'm about to come get you."

"Alright, I'll be ready."

"Be outside."

"Outside? Bitch it's the dead of winter. I'll be in the hallway. Blow your horn."

20 minutes later

We arrived on 84th and Marquette. The police had the car surrounded. Heidi's ass jumped out before I could even park. She took off running towards Jaw's car. I tried to hurry up and park; because once I saw the officer stop her, I knew that there was about to be some shit.

"Ma'am, you can't go over there. This is a crime scene."

"This ain't no motherfucking crime scene. That's my son's stolen car. Move out of my way before I move you."

"Are you threatening me?"

I called Ashley.

"Please hurry up and get here because Heidi's about to go to jail."

"For what?"

No sooner than she asked that . . . WHAM! Heidi knocked the police officer clean out. I shook my head.

"Assault on a police officer."

"Shit! I'm on the way."

Jaw

I was thinking, "Was this bitch really about to get away with this?" I had been in this basement for a week now. My dick was so raw from her sucking and fuck on it. I prayed every night that she jumped on my dick that she didn't get pregnant. Every time I nutted, she jumped on my dick. Her pussy was like a Hoover vacuum. It sucked up every drop. If I got loose, I swear I was going to kill that bitch. She had this shit planned for a while. When I needed to use the restroom or wash my ass, she'd uncuff me while holding a Taser to me. I tried her the first time and she shocked me so bad I had the shakes for a few days. I had to play the nice-guy role. She started leaving me untied when she left. When she's there, she tied me up and lay in the bed with me. I guess she must have read my mind. The girl had problems. Every five minutes she was telling me that she loved me. I had to suck it up and say it back.

"If you keep acting right, I'll let you come upstairs where you belong."

"It's cool. Take your time, ma. It is what it is. When you're ready, and then let me know."

"Thank you for understanding me and coming around. I just want us to be together. Let me show you that I'm the better woman for you."

"Okay, boo, do you."

This shit was going to take a minute.

"Where my chain?"

"You don't need it. We are trying to start a new life. Let's let the past be the past."

What? I was fuming on the inside. Do you know how much I paid for that chain? Stupid-ass bitch!

EIGHTEEN

Mia

One week later

I had to set my auntie straight. After I told her everything that happened, she quickly jumped sides. Yeah, you know I had to put my lil' twist on a few things. Little Ms. JoJo had her fooled. She failed to tell her that them motherfucker killed Boogie, Jr., and Ramone. Cee was pissed. In the end, I accomplished my goal. I didn't even know that Uncle T's daughter, Spooky, was even in the city. I planned on hollering at her. For now I was just glad to be in the company of my man who, by the way, has been behaving really well. He was gaining my trust and making me love him even more.

Like today, I was in a bad-ass mood. I was tired of selling drugs with no help. True enough, I had some loyal-ass niggas that copped from me, but I wanted to expand and

I couldn't do that without a team. When I went downstairs to check on him, he was laying in the bed watching T.V. and eating popcorn. I kind of felt bad for keeping him locked up. He needed to be on the same page with me if I was going to let his ass out of the basement.

"What's good, baby? Come here and give daddy a kiss."

Damn I loved this boy. I prayed that he stayed like this. I mean two weeks under constant lock and key was enough.

"Baby I'm sad."

"Why you sad, Lovely?"

"I'm tired of hustling by myself. I mean the money is great, but damn I need a break. I can't keep doing this shit full time without no help."

"You smart, boo. You'll figure something out. Come lay down and let's take a nap."

I uncuffed his other arm and let him hold me.

"If I let you outta this basement, will you promise not to leave me?"

His whole life depended on him answering this question right.

"Man, ma, I gotchu. At first I hated you, but after I sat back and thought about all the shit we been through, I know you love me. I need that real love in my life. I'ma show you that I'm the man you want in your life. I love you Mia."

Yes, gah damn it . . . yes. He said the right shit. I'm sure after two weeks of putting this A-1 pussy on him, he'd finally come around.

"Let's go upstairs."

Jaw

I thought that I wasn't going to be able to survive this shit mentally. I ain't never hated nobody the way I hated this bitch. I'm one of them niggas that cannot fake shit. I swear I should win an Oscar for my award-winning performance.

I quit underestimating that bitch, too. I haven't tried shit that could potentially get me killed. That girl was unstable for real. I knew my family was going crazy. I had to find a way to let them know I was good.

Door Unlocking

Mia came in the room looking all sad and shit. Lights, camera, action!

"What's good, baby? Come here and give daddy a kiss."

"Baby, I'm sad."

I knew what she wanted. I just had to play it cool and comfort her. Once she explained why she was sad, I knew this was my one chance to gain her trust. Not only could I gain her trust, but I could get paid in the process. What? You're probably thinking . . . how could I be thinking about money at a time like this right? Because after I kill this bitch, it's still money out there to be made.

"If I let you out of the basement, will you promise not to leave me?"

Got her! I was going to play it cool; but when I got what I needed from her ass, it was lights out bitch!

NINETEEN

Young Meech

I can't believe the big homie has been missing for this along. Poohman been on beast mode. I ain't never seen that nigga that mad.

Ring, Ring

I looked at my phone and saw that it was Money Man.

"Yo, bruh!"

"Nigger, get over here ASAP!"

"What's wrong? We got beef?"

"This crackhead named Freddie just came and tried to sell Jaw's chain."

"WHAT? Where he get it from?"

"He said some hoe down the street on 42nd walked up to him and gave it to him."

"I'm on my way. Don't move 'til I get there."

20 minutes later

I walked in the spot ready for action.

"Money, don't you think we should call Boo and yo momma?"

"For what? We got this. The nigga in the basement."

When we walked down stairs, I couldn't hold the laugh that busted out of my mouth. Outlaw was a little terror. He was down there slapping the shit out of the old man.

"Shut up! *Slap* Punk ass nigga! *Slap..* You better not be lying." *Slap, Slap*

"Man, Outlaw, fall back, killa."

I walked up to the old man who looked like he was about to have a heart attack. When he saw me, he started pleading his cases.

"I swear, Young, I didn't steal the chain. The girl gave it to me."

"Can you take us to the crib?"

"Yes, please just don't let that lil' nigga slap me no more. My gah damn face hurt!" *Slap.*

"Shut up, nigga."

Me and Money Man fell out laughing.

"Chill, Outlaw. Untie him. Don't try no funny shit, Freddie."

We all jumped in my truck and drove down to 42nd street. As soon as I hit the block, I asked Freddie to show me where the crib was.

"It's red and white."

I was about to say something until I heard . . . *Slap.*

"All these houses red and white, mothafucker."

Outlaw slapped the poor man again.

"You gotta do better than. that. What else you remember?"

"It was a black Lexus in the drive way."

I looked at Money Man.

"Do you know what type of car she drives?"

"I know it's black. That's all I remember. You know I smoke hella weed. I can barely remember the days of the week, Young."

We decided to park in the middle of the block and wait. Freddie started rocking back and forth getting on my nerves.

"Quit fucking rocking, dude!"

"I need my fix. Let me get a dub, Young?"

"Outlaw, give him a dub."

When Outlaw gave him the work, I couldn't believe that nigga whipped out his crack pipe and was about to flame up.

"Whoa, what the fuck? Get the fuck out."

"Oh, I didn't know you didn't need me." *Slap*

Outlaw slapped him the back of his head so hard that his head bounced off of the window. "Damn," was all I could say. He jumped out and ran into a house not too far from where we were parked. I knew this was going to be a long day.

"Money Man, roll something."

I figured I'd play catch-up with my crew since we ain't been kicking it like that.

"Money, what's good, bruh?"

"Shit, chasing that almighty dollar. The spot over here been juking."

"That's what's up. You paid all the runners yet?"

"I'ma do it tomorrow before we re-up."

"Where yo girl?"

"She been hanging out with her cousin. I think her name JoJo or something like that."

Did I hear him right?

"You say JoJo? What does she look like?"

"I ain't never seen her, but aww shit I forgot to ask you something. Do you know some nigga name Big T that ran Englewood?"

I looked at Money Man with some suspicious eyes.

Why the fuck was he asking me about that pussy-ass nigga? I never told Money Man or Outlaw about that Thanksgiving night.

"What about him?"

Money Man sensed my sudden change of mood.

"Damn nigga, chill. I was asking because Spooky said the he was her father."

I dropped my head. You have got to be fucking kidding me. This world was indeed too small. My mind started to race. Was this nigga out to get me, too? Was he going to ride with his bitch? He couldn't be. He didn't know. I had to tell him.

"Yeah, I know that nigga, Big T. He had my father killed."

I could tell he didn't know the history. His mouth dropped open and he almost dropped the blunt.

"Nigga, tell me you lying."

"I'm not. I didn't kill Big T. Poohman did. I killed his bitch who, by the way, happened to be my mother."

Outlaw whipped his head around and gave me the craziest look.

"Yo momma?"

"Hell yeah. That bitch played a part in my father's death. They both had to go!"

I looked Money Man dead in the eyes and said, "So now that you know your bitch is the enemy, what's good?"

"Nigga, I'ma Chi City boy all day. She not in the city for no reason. I think she said her cousin JoJo got a baby daddy named Lil Man that she . . ."

"Nigga, if that's the JoJo I think it is; this shit is bigger than all of us. JoJo fucking with the same Lil Man that killed my sister and my auntie. But I'ma 'bout to fuck yo head all the way up. Remember the nigga Big Moe that got robbed by Ju, Re, and Dirty?"

"Yeah, Jaw told me about that nigga."

"That's her fucking cousin. So if Spooky is JoJo's cousin, you do the math!"

He was speechless.

"You know her Auntie Cee is the one giving us the work for the low-low? Plus, Spooky's lil' slick ass been stealing work on the side, too."

"You gon' have to WHACK! that bitch."

"I gotchu. After we find my brother, it's a done deal."

Damn, I hope we find Jaw . . . and fast. You never know who is who around this motherfucker.

TWENTY

Boo

"Officer, please don't lock my sister up, we are under enough stress."

"Well, she should have thought about that before she punched my partner. Her ass is going to jail."

That gah damn Heidi. This shit has gots to stop. I was about to call Ashley back when she pulled up. Thank you Jesus! She got out of the car and walked right past me to the other squad car, said a few words, and that was that. I could tell the officer was pissed.

"Let her out of the car."

"But Serg!"

"LET HER OUT NOW!"

After the officer let Heidi out of the car and uncuffed her, they pulled off. Ashley looked at Heidi and rolled her eyes.

"You cannot hit my officers, Heidi . . . period!"

"Bitch, that's my son's car. He's missing, and I'm under slot of stress. I needed to release some built-up anger. My bad."

"I don't care. You can't hit the police!"

"Why not? They shoot us black folks for no reason."

When we finally made our way over to Jaw's car, the inside was a mess. Food wrappers and pop cans were all over the place. I knew that something was wrong then because Jaw never left his car like that.

Phone ringing

We each checked our phones. It was coming from the backseat. I got in the back seat and looked around on the floor. Bingo! I found his phone under a Wendy's bag.

"Heidi, don't you still have a key to Jaw's car?"

"No, he took it back when I stole his car and went to St. Louis."

I picked up my phone and called JuJu.

"Ju?"

"Yeah, Boo."

"We found Jaw's car around the corner from E's house. Do you have a spare key?"

"Yeah, I'm at E's now. I'ma 'bout to come outside."

Not even three minutes later, Ju came outside and gave us some much-needed motivation.

"Is his phone in the car?"

I was kind of reluctant to give it to her. I mean, this was still my nephew. I didn't really know what the fuck he had going on. She saw right through me.

"Boo, I'm not trying to be all in his business. Young told me that Jaw was recording him and Mia's conversations."

Damn, I felt stupid. I handed her the phone, and she went straight to the recording device on his phone.

"See, look, the date it was recorded is right here."

She pointed to the screen

"This was the last conversation that was recorded. It's Valentine's Day."

She pressed play: "What's up?"

"Hey baby, where are we meeting at?"

"Let me come to your crib and chill for a minute."

"We could do that. Just pick me up something to drink."

"What's your address?"

"4231 Princeton."

"I'm on my way."

Ju, Heidi, Ashley, and I stood frozen for a several moments. I couldn't believe what we heard. We knew where he was. Now it was time to form a plan. How the hell were we going to get him out of there?"

"We should just go kick in the bitch's door!"

I was known to do a little door-kicking back in my gang-banging days. Ashley shook her head.

"I think that's the best way to go. If you call the police, they gon' get all up in your business."

Heidi had a crazy-ass look on her face. It kinda scared me.

"Heidi, call Money Man and Outlaw."

She walked off to make the call. I couldn't help but eavesdrop on the call. She was getting all hyped and shit. She ran back over to us.

"Money Man, Young, Meech, and Outlaw are over on that block right now. Some cluck tried to sell them Jaw's chain he got from some girl. He told them where to find her but didn't know the exact house she came out of. Let's suit up and go get my boy!"

"We not about to get over there and make a scene. Let's do this as quietly as we possibly can."

I saw JuJu looking like she was able to cry.

"What's wrong?"

"I'ma kill that bitch. Let's go!"

Well, alrighty then!

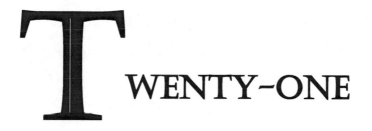WENTY-ONE

ReRe

It had been cold in this house and I wasn't talking about the weather. Poohman been on ice mode ever since Jaw came up missing. I didn't know how to get through to him either. Shit, he was always the lovey-dovey one. I had to try and defrost his ass.

"Poohman, come here."

"Na, you come here. I'm busy."

Huh? Damn, cracked my face. He ain't never talked to me like that. When I walked in the living room, he was laying on the couch.

"Really?"

"What Re? I'm not in the mood for nothing right now. My best friend is missing, and I want to kill something!"

He wasn't mad, he was hurting.

"Baby, let's go for a ride. Maybe we can just hit the expressway and . . . *Ring, Ring.*

I was so glad my phone rang. It was Ju. I started not to answer it, but when Poohman gave me that 'who the fuck is that' look. I knew better.

"Ju, what's good? WHAT? We are on our way."

I hung up and grabbed my shoes.

"Bay, come on, they know where Jaw is."

He jumped up so fast I didn't even realize that he already had his shoes on.

"Was you laying on the couch with your shoes on?"

The look he gave me shut me the fuck up . . . quick! He snatched my keys from me.

"I'm driving."

Lil Man

I knew my joy-riding days were over when I saw the police car pull up behind Jaw's car. Fuck! It was too cold to be walking. I had to steal another car. My mission wasn't all bad. I finally saw JoJo. She was indeed staying with Dirty. I wasn't going to kill her just yet, but Dirty was about to die.

JuJu

My heart was racing the whole time we were driving. My man had been gone for over two weeks. What the fuck was she doing to him? Did he have sex with her? Is he even still alive? I realized at that very moment that if he was still alive, we were going to make our relationship work. I didn't know how much I loved him until all this bullshit started happening. I was so lost in my thoughts that I didn't know that we were already on 42nd. I looked at Boo and waited for her to make a move.

"What's the plan?"

"You are going to stay put. Heidi is going to stay put with you."

Heidi looked at me and I saw the relief all over her face. I almost laughed.

"Don't worry, me and Ju gon' be right here when ya'll get back."

I wasn't feeling that shit at all. I was about to say what was on my mind until Boo gave me her infamous stank face.

"Just bring him out safely."

Young Meech

"Hello Boo? What's the verdict?"

"Put me on speaker phone."

I did as I was told

"You on?"

"Okay, we found Jaw's phone, and he did record all his conversations he had with that girl. We got am address."

I saw the look of death when I looked at Outlaw. He was ready. It was time to finally lay that hoe, Mia, down.

"Well what's the address?" She started laughing.

"Ya'll sitting right in front of the house . . . 4231. Outlaw, you and Money Man are going to go through the back. Meech, meet me at the front door. Poohman and Re are at the end of the block, and Heidi and Ju right behind ya'll."

I looked at my crew and said, "Let's go get our boy."

Mia

I thought I was making a mistake letting Jaw out of the basement. To my surprise, he didn't make a run for it. He actually went upstairs, took a shower, and got in the bed. I was so happy that he was on my page now.

"Baby, you hungry?"

"Make me a steak and some cheese eggs."

"Anything else?"

"Yeah, come suck my dick before you go."

Now that's what I'm talking about. I climbed on top of my man and gave him the best head of his life.

Jaw

My heart was racing the second she let me out of that dungeon. I had to play it cool if my plan was going to work. I walked right passed the front door, went upstairs, and headed straight for the bathroom like I owned the place. She made sure my draws and socks were on the bed when I got out of the shower. I let the hot water beat my body up. I didn't realize that I was crying until I looked in the mirror. My eyes were bloodshot red. It wasn't tears of sadness. I was angry. I wanted to kill that bitch. I knew that my girl was hurting. I had to be careful. I knew she had some shit up her sleeves. After my shower, I turned on Sports Center and lay in the bed.

"Baby you hungry?"

After I told he what I wanted, I had a little fun with her mouth. The hoe's head game was lethal. Too bad she was a dead bitch walking.

Mia

I sucked my man's dick until I heard his toes pop, and then I went downstairs to fix him dinner. I had to make sure that he was on his best behavior first. I went into the pantry and moved a can of peas. Once I did, the wall moved to the side revealing my security room full of cameras. Jaw might have thought that shit was sweet. Not just yet, baby. I had a camera in every room of this house—even the bathroom! I knew how many turds he dropped when he shit. I also had cameras all around the outside of my house. I zoomed in on two familiar faces walking through my gangway.

"What the fuck?"

Did he call them? How? He didn't have a phone. Shit! If those two bastards are here, I know they brought company.

TWENTY-TWO

Lil Mama

"Can I ask you a question?"

"Yeah, ma, what's on your mind?"

"What do you really do for a living?"

I could tell that question caught her off guard.

"Man, Lil Mama, you ain't no dummy. I took over my brother's empire. I also been taking care of his daughter, Spooky."

"I'm only asking because I don't wanna be laying up with no stranger."

Something wasn't right with Cee. Her phone would ring all hours of the night. If it was money like she said, why not answer? She don't even pick up for me on the weekends. Is there really a niece? She had me ready to get my Sherlock Holmes on.

"Cee, you not on no bullshit with me are you? I would hate to have to turn into a psycho dike."

She started laughing like I was playing. Little did she know I was 'bout that life.

"Man, Lil Mama, you tripping. Don't start looking for some shit that ain't there."

Her phone started ringing. When she looked at me, I mugged the fuck out of her.

"Answer your phone before I punch the shit out of you."

She actually answered it.

"Hey sexy. What you doing? I miss you too. I'm 'bout to come see you right now."

She hung up and smiled at me.

"What?"

"You real funny."

Little did I know that the joke was about to be on me.

JoJo

I was going on four months and could no longer hide it. My little girl was growing at a rapid pace. I even began feeling slight movements. I was so blessed to have E with me. She has been my rock, not to mention the help and support I was getting from my cousin, Spooky. I hadn't seen or heard from Lil Man. I was happy about that shit. He was going to eventually become a problem. I knew that he wasn't just going to let me and my baby live happily ever after. I was prepared. I was also relieved that Re's crazy ass ain't been over here either. I didn't need the extra stress. E was all I had right now.

"E, you wanna go see a movie? I'm bored."

"Hell naw. You know how much it cost to go see a movie? We can find my bootlegger Wish over there on the Dan Ryan. He got some new shit."

"Ole cheap ass. Come on. I want some McDonald's, too."

"You giving up some ass tonight? You know what they say about a good ole pregnant cat?"

"You wish. I'll drown yo ass in all these juices."

"You might be right. Let me play wit'cha booty then."

"Fuck no, nasty. Come on, I'm hungry."

Lil Man

I thought it was going to be hard staking out Dirty's crib, but it really wasn't. I stole a car when I went out west to get KeeKee.

"Pass the weed, nigga." *Giggling*

"Man, don't start all that giggling and shit."

"When you lace the weed, I can't help it. It tickles."

"Something is seriously wrong with you."

I was about to say something when my words got caught in my throat. Dirty and JoJo walked out of the house hand in hand. They looked like a happy couple. KeeKee zoomed in on what I was looking at and made matters worse.

"Damn, cuzzo, ain't that'cha baby mama?"

"Yeah, man!"

"And ain't that the nigga that was shooting at us? Yo, bitch set us up. I told you, but you ain't wanna listen. What type of hoes you be dealing with?"

As he was talking, I grew madder and madder.

"Shut the fuck up and follow them."

"Why can't we get 'em right here?"

"Na, we need to get them away from the hood. We don't know where them other hoes at. Just follow them."

I was going to kill that bitch, Dirty, tonight. JoJo was coming with me. We followed them all the way to 87th and State. I saw some fat-ass dude run up to their car with some DVDs.

"So what the fuck they tryin' do? Make it a Blockbuster night?"

KeeKee knew how to egg me on.

"Looks like it. Damn, Joe, you let a bitch take yo girl?"

I didn't even respond. After they drove off, they went across the street to the McDonald's. It was time to end their little date night.

"KeeKee, park over there by the alley."

"Man, cuzzo go handle yo business. Let that hoe know you run this."

"Don't call her no hoe. That's my baby mama. Show some respect."

"Mothafucker really? She almost had us killed. She with the enemy right now. Respect my dick! Handle your business before I get mad."

When I got out of the car, the cold air woke up all my senses. The coke from the weed had me feeling like I was Tony Montana. I had to make sure my aim was on point. After JoJo had my baby, she was a dead bitch, too. Tonight was Dirty's time to die. I ran around the back of the McDonalds when I saw them pull up to the drive-thru window. I had to wait a few minutes because there were a few cars in front of them. When they finally got to the front of the line, I made my move.

JoJo

"Welcome to McDonald's, may I take your order?"

I never got a chance to give the lady my damn order. I looked in the driver-side mirror and saw a nigga in a hoodie running towards the car. I almost shit myself when I saw Lil Man's face. The nigga was actually smiling.

"E . . . GUN!"

BOC!, BOC!, BOC!, BOC!, BOC!

I tried to throw the car in gear and pull off, but I just really learned how to drive. My whip game wasn't that proper. I rammed the car in front of us.

"I'm trying to, E."

The bullets were steady flying nonstop. How many fucking guns did he have?

"AWW SHIT, JOJO, I'M HIT! JoJo, drive this fucking car before he kills us, man!

I was about to have a fucking stroke. E was bleeding from her upper chest area. I didn't want a bullet to hit me in the head, so my head was low. I swerved out of the parking lot, whacking a few cars in the process.

"Take me to the nearest hospital, JoJo."

"Where you hit at, boo?"

"My shoulder. Take me to Jackson Park Hospital on 76th and Stoney Island."

How did he know that we were going to be at that McDonald's? Now I gotta explain shit to her friends. Shit!

TWENTY-THREE

Money Man

"Alright, Boo, we are in position. It's cameras everywhere. If she's in there, then she already knows that we're here.

"Me and Meech are at the front door. As soon as you hang up the phone, kick that mothafucking door in. Be careful."

I hung up the phone and looked at my little brother.

"Outlaw, you ready? On three, we both gon' kick this bitch in."

"I'm ready."

"One, two, three."

Mia

Fuck! I ran to the living room to grab my AK-47 up under the couch. I was about to kill everybody. I'ma kill Jaw's ass last. I'm sick of his meddling-ass family. As soon as I grabbed my gun, I heard my backdoor fly open.

CLICK, CLACK

"Come on in here, mothafuckers."

Boo

"A'ight Meech . . . One, two, three!"

BOOM!

Meech kicked the door off of its hinges. As soon as the door came flying open, I saw a woman running towards the back of the house.

"Meech, go get here. I'ma look for Jaw."

I quickly hit the basement and looked in every room. I almost threw up when I saw the red room. Jaw's pictures covered every wall in that room. There was a big-ass red bed in the room with cuffs all over the place. We were dealing with a sick bitch. I tripped over something at the foot of the bed.

"What the fuck?"

My heart rate sped up when I realized it was my nephew's boot. Where the fuck was he?

BOC!, BOC!, BOC!, BOC!

"Oh no! I ran up outta that basement so fast, you woulda thought it was on fire.

"Meech, where you at?"

He didn't answer.

BOC!, BOC!, BOC!

It was coming from the kitchen. When I went to investigate, I saw Money Man and Outlaw shooting the wall.

"Why the fuck are ya'll shooting at the wall?"

"Because, Auntie, Outlaw said she ran in the pantry. We can't get in there because she locked the door."

"Stay here."

Jaw

I waited a good 10 minutes after she went downstairs to start going through her shit. In her closet, she had a gang of men's clothing on one side. Something told me to just check the sizes. All the sizes from the shirts to the pants were my size. Man I had to get the fuck out of here. God must have heard my prayers, because the next thing I know it sounded like World War 3 downstairs.

BOC!, BOC!, BOC!, BOC!

When I heard them four gun shots, I grabbed a shirt and a pair of pants to throw on. Whoever was downstairs shooting wasn't about to catch me slipping in my draws and socks. On the way out of the closet, I grabbed a pair of all

Black Timbs. I didn't even check to see if they fit. I already knew they did. I threw the boots on and ran to the bedroom door. I didn't have a phone to call for help or a gun to help my damn self. Whatever the case was, I wasn't about to go out like no punk-ass nigga. I looked around the room for something. On the night stand was a big-ass candle. Yeah, a candle. I know what you probably thinking, but check this out. It wasn't one of them little Family Dollar candles. It was one of them big ones from Bath and Body Works. Hey it was something. I found a good-ass hiding spot on top of the dresser behind the door. Whoever came in that door was getting the shit bust to the white meat. Seconds later, I heard somebody running up the stairs. When the door opened, I held my breath and got ready.

Young Meech

After I kicked in the front door, I saw the back half of a female running towards the kitchen.

"Meech, go get her."

I didn't waste time trying to catch that bitch. As soon as I hit the corner . . .

WHAM!

I ran smack dead into Money Man.

"Damn, Money, look out. Where the bitch go?"

"I saw her run in that pantry."

Outlaw's crazy ass walked up to the door and opened fire.

"I'm about to check upstairs. Don't let that hoe creep up out of that closet."

I ran up the stairs as fast as I could. I was praying that my homie was alright. I searched two rooms that were right off of the stairs. Nothing! There was one more room to check. I was scared as hell, too. I didn't know what I was gonna find. I opened the door slowly. When I walked all the way in the room, I caught something out of the corner of my eye. I swung my gun around prepared to shoot, when all of a sudden Jaw screamed, "MEECH, DON'T SHOOT!"

"Nigga ,why the fuck you hiding behind the door?"

BOC!, BOC!, BOC!

"Because I didn't know what the fuck was going on. Who the fuck is still down there shooting?"

"Probably yo damn brothers. Let's get the fuck outta here before the police come."

We took off running out of the room and ran into Boo.

"Gah damn it. Ya'll scared me. Nephew, you a'ight?"

"Hell yeah. Where's that crazy bitch at?"

"Don't know. She ran when we kicked in the door. Let's go now!"

After we made it up outta the house, Money Man and Outlaw came running from the back.

"Why ya'll running? What's that smell?"

"Well the bitch never came out of the closet so we kinda set the kitchen on fire."

"Man, ya'll crazy as hell. Jaw, you riding with us?"

"No the fuck he a'int!"

JuJu walked up on us with a mean-ass look on her face. Jaw knew what time it was. He turned to me and shook my hand.

"I'ma call you later, my nigga."

I heard the police sirens and knew what time it was . . . time to bounce.

WENTY-FOUR

Lil Mama

"Well, why the fuck didn't you call me?"

"Bitch, I did. You didn't answer your phone."

"I ain't got no missed calls from you. Fuck all that, is he alright?"

"He's fine. We didn't find that bitch though. She got away."

"Damn, that's crazy. "

"Lil Mama, what's going on with you?"

"Girl, my boo got me tripping. I don't trust her ass. I really think she fucking around."

"Then leave that hoe alone. We gotta get these kids in line. Enough is enough. We need to set better examples. Bitch, I'm not trying to go back to jail."

"And you think I am? Let's do what we said we were gonna do."

"You still wanna do the night club?"

"Yes. We can do this. Think about it. But for now, let's sit down with the kids and get their minds right. If they do summer school, they can graduate on time."

"That's the plan, Boo. Let me hit you back. My boo on the other line."

"Yeah, whatever. You better get ya mind right. I'm 'bout to call Ashley to see if that shooting was reported."

Ashley

Thank goodness it was Friday. Today, my boo was picking me up and we were going out.

(Ring, Ring)

"Hey, boo, how did everything go?"

"Shit I was calling to ask you. Did anybody call talking about a shootout on 42nd and Princeton?"

"Um, I think I heard about a house catching fire after a domestic dispute. Did ya'll find him?"

"Yeah, we good. Thank you for not letting Heidi get locked up."

"Tell her she better not hit another one of my officers. If she do, her ass is going to jail."

"What you doing tonight? Wanna go have some drinks?"

"Me and my boo supposed to hit a few bars down town."

"Your boo? Okay then. Me and Heidi might find you."

"Alright, see you tonight."

JuJu

I was unusually nervous around my own damn man. After we got home, he went straight to the bathroom and ran a bath. I had so many questions I was just too afraid to ask. I wanted to know if he fucked her. Sad to say, but that was the only thing I was really thinking about.

"Ju, come take a bath with me."

"I don't want to. As a matter of fact, turn the water off. We need to talk now!"

He did as I asked and came and sat next to me. I wanted to throw up. I smelled her scent all over him. He saw me turn my nose up, so he scooted over.

"So what happened? How the fuck did she get the upper hand on you like that?"

He put his head in his hands and took a deep breath. I knew that after this conversation, our relationship would never be the same.

"And I wanna know everything."

After nearly two hours, I was in tears. My lil' feelings were so hurt. I couldn't breathe. It felt like my heart was ripped out of my chest. All he could do was hold me as I had a meltdown. I couldn't believe that crazy bitch tied him up and raped him repeatedly. The hardest thing to accept now was that there is a chance that she could be pregnant.

"So what you wanna do, Ju? She not gonna go away. If she ends up pregnant, please don't leave me."

"Do you want . . . well, let me say this, if she does get pregnant, what are you gonna do?"

"I don't wanna think about that. If I see her, I'ma kill her. Baby or not. We together for life, ma."

I had to accept it. I loved this man, through thick and thin. I hoped death didn't do us part.

(Ring, Ring)

Jaw snatched my phone. "Damn, why you do that?"

"Hello?"

"Um, can I speak to JuJu?"

"Who is this?"

"Jaw?"

"Yeah, who is this?"

"This JoJo."

"What the fuck you want?"

Who was he talking to?

"Give me my phone."

I snatched it from him and walked off.

"Why the fuck is JoJo calling you?"

"Because she can. What's good, JoJo?"

"Me and E went to McDonald's last night and out of nowhere Lil Man came up shooting. E got shot."

My stomach dropped. If it ain't one thing it's another. Jaw saw the look on my face and ran over to me.

"What's wrong, baby?"

"JoJo, where ya'll at?"

"At Jackson Park Hospital. Look, she's okay. It was a shoulder wound. She's doped up on pain meds. Her mother is up here cussing everybody out in Creole."

"We're on the way."

"When you get here I'ma leave, because I don't want to be near ReRe. My lil' cousin is on her way to get me in a cab."

"Thank you."

When I hung up the phone, Jaw had the nerve to be giving me the ugly face.

"Why the fuck is she calling you?"

"Come on. I'll tell you in the car."

TWENTY-FIVE

Boo

"Sis, you wanna come out and have a few drinks with me?"

"I don't know, Boo. Every time we go out, we got one foot in jail and the other one dangling in the graveyard."

I started cracking up because she was dead serious.

"It's all good, sis. We chilling tonight. So go on and get all dressed. It's a ladies night."

"Alrighty then. I'm breaking out my cat suit. It got diamonds and glitter all over it, too. Girl, hurry up and come get me."

I hung up and called Lil Mama to see if she wanted to go. No answer. I wasn't about to kiss her bony ass. Let me go put on my freak 'um dress. I might find my future tonight.

Three hours later, we were sipping Ace of Spade at this club called Adriana's, enjoying my cousin Zona, Man, and Future rip the stage. Heidi was having a ball.

"You see, Boo, this is my idea of a good time. No drama! You did good, sis. You think I can get Future to take me with him tonight? I know he'll like all this thickness, unlike his bony-ass baby mama Clara."

I spit my drink all over the floor. My sister was crazy, but I loved every minute of it.

"Oh, Boo, look, there goes Ashley. Oh my, I'm not gay, but look at what she got on her arm. Cute huh?"

Yeah Ashley had a cutie on her arm tonight. All right, Ash, get it bitch. I waved my hand in the air to get her attention. She gave us both hugs. My girl was glowing.

"Well who is this, Ash?"

"Heidi . . . Boo, this is my boo, Carmen."

"Hey ladies, how ya'll doing?"

After the introduction, Carmen went to the bar to get us another round.

"Damn Ash, nice one."

The four of us had a ball. Carmen was a good match for her. She was a perfect gentle woman. I saw her phone ring several times. She never bothered to answer it. All her attention was on my friend. I was happy for her.

"Ash, you look good, girl."

"I feel good, too. I didn't think I would date again so soon, but you know."

"Yeah, we know. Lil Mama got a boo, too. I tried to get her to come out, but she was in her mood so . . ."

"I'm glad she didn't come. I'm not really feeling her like that."

"Are you still mad about that shit?"

"Yeah I am. No matter if she meant well or not, I suffered in that basement. I just can't let that go."

"Alright then. Let's enjoy the rest of our night."

The night ended without Heidi knocking somebody out. Thank you, Jesus!

Lil Mama

"You got the nerve to not answer the phone for me? Fuck you, Cee!"

I was on fire. That bitch called me and told me to get ready to go out, and now she didn't want to pick up the phone? Oh bitch, you must not know 'bout me. I took a shower and went to bed. Carmen had me fucked all the way up.

Next Day

Ring, Ring

Well look who's calling. It was Carmen.

"What the fuck you want?"

"Whoa, that's how you wanna start the day?"

"Don't worry about how I start my day. You fucked up my night."

"I'm downstairs. Open the door before I kick it in."

"Yeah a'ight."

After I opened the door, I thought about bussing her ass in her eye.

"So what happened to you last night?"

"Man, you know my job is demanding. Go get dressed. I'm about to take you and my niece to lunch."

I hurried up and took my shower. I was ready to meet this niece.

Spooky

Things were almost back to normal. After they found Jaw, Money Man got right back to the money. I was tweaking when I heard that my cousin, Mia, was the one responsible for kidnapping Jaw. That bitch crazy. I been spending a lot of time with JoJo lately. My Auntie Carmen wanted me to stop talking to her after Mia told her all that bullshit, but I wasn't. I'ma do what the fuck I wanna do. Today my auntie was taking me and her new boo to lunch.

I did notice that Money Man ain't been the same with me since his brother's kidnapping. He's been real distant. The only time he really said anything to me was when he needed me to hit up my auntie for some more work. Today was no different. No kiss or hug . . . nothing!

"I'm about to leave. Can I have a kiss?"

"Naw, I ain't in the mood for no kiss."

See?

"What the fuck is your problem?"

"Ain't got one. Don't you got somewhere to be?"

Fuck him. I wasn't about to kiss his ass.

Money Man

In the back of my mind, I always knew something wasn't right with that girl. Damn shame she was on the wrong side. I called Young Meech to set things in motion.

"Yo, whud up boy?"

"Shit, what's cracking?"

"What'chu wanna do about shorty?"

"Make her rob her auntie, then rock her ass to sleep. We need that work though. You a'ight with that?"

"Man, there's a million hoes out there. I'm sure I can find one that ain't related to our enemy."

"After I clean out my crib, we can do a little spring cleaning of our own."

TWENTY-SIX

Lil Mama

I felt kind of dumb for doubting Cee. Lunch with her and her niece was really nice. She truly loved that lil' girl. It reminded me of the relationship I got with JuJu. Things have slowly but surely been falling back in place. The three stooges have been on their school work. We thought that it would be best if they were all home-schooled. Once they caught up, they'd finish the rest of the year at school. Young Meech was another story. He was falling deeper and deeper into those Kingpin shoes. His attitude was changing. I was starting to get worried. You would have never thought that he was just 15 years old. I figured it was time for us to clean out Shawn's stuff.

Ring, Ring

It was Boo's crazy ass.

"Yeah, sis."

"Aww shit, you answered the phone for me?"

"Fuck you."

"Wha'chu 'bout to do?"

"Go help Meech pack up Shawn's things. You wanna come?"

"Yeah, I think I can help. Yo ass shoulda came out with me and Heidi. We met up with Ashley and her new boo. Girl, we had a ball."

"I ain't miss shit. You know that girl ain't fucking with me like that. Shill in her feelings about that bullshit. Maybe me, you, and Heidi can go out this weekend. I was in my chest last night anyway. My girl been walking on thin ice We good now, though. Let's see how long that shit last. I would have to see this new boo of Ashley's though. Is she cute?"

"Hell yeah. I'ma meet you at Shawn's. I'm about to leave now."

One hour later

We were all joking and laughing, trying to lighten the mood. It was real emotional going through Shawn's things. Young Meech was doing the best he could at holding it together. He usually didn't smoke his weed around me, but today I made an exception. I saw a few tears when we got to the box that held Young Meech's daddy's things.

"Ma, look at me when I was a shorty."

He was as cute as he wanted to be. King was holding Meech and his mom was off to the side. The expression on her face didn't read happiness. It looked like she was jealous of the joy King shared with his son. There were a few pictures of King and Tank as well. Meech snatched the one I was looking at and attempted to rip it.

"No, don't do that."

"Why Ma? He had my father killed."

"Good or bad, it was a part of his life. Just know that King was a beast. T was a pussy-ass nigga. He couldn't kill King. He had to have another nigga do it."

While I was trying to comfort my baby, Boo's ass was tweaking off some other pictures.

"Damn, this world is really small."

"What the hell are you talking about?"

"Here is Ashley's new boo in the picture with King and Tank."

"Oh yeah? Let me see."

When she gave me that picture, I took the blunt my son had and took a deep pull. Yeah, I was still on parole, but I couldn't believe my eyes. She saw the look on my face and came to my aide.

"What the fuck is your problem? You can't smoke. What's wrong?"

"That lying bitch! This . . ." I pointed "is my girlfriend, Cee."

Boo just stared at me.

"Bitch, is you sure?"

"You don't think I would know my bitch?"

"Man, ma, what you fussing about? Let me see what you talking about."

I handed her the picture and started pacing. I noticed Meech was shaking his head.

"What boy? Say something."

"You fucking Carmen?"

I was shocked that he even knew her name. I said Cee not Carmen.

"How you know her name?"

"This bitch is Tank's sister."

Me and Boo were stuck. She grabbed the blunt from me and lit it.

He continued, "I'm about to fuck ya'll head up even more. The lil' bitch that Money Man is fucking is Tank's daughter."

"That little girl, Spooky?"

Damn we just had lunch two weeks ago.

I was speechless.

"So you mean to tell me that not only am I fucking the enemy, but the bitch is a cheater too?"

Boo was in deep thought.

"Lil Mama, this shit has got to stop. We can't let nobody take down what we've worked so hard to build."

"Boo, you right. Me and Money Man already had a plan to make Spooky show us where her auntie kept her work at. After that, we was gonna pop her ass."

I was with that plan, sneaky-ass bitch. Probably got it from her auntie.

"Well, Ashley asked me to come out with her and her boo. Wanna show up and show out?"

"Absolutely."

"Ma, don't give away the fact that we know who she really is. Let shit settle before we make that big move. Okay?"

"You asking for too much. I'll try."

TWENTY-SEVEN

Dirty E

Ten weeks later

I had been laying extremely low ever since that mothafucker shot me. Ohhhwweee . . . when I get right, that nigga's ass was mine. I couldn't stay at my crib because I was almost a hundred percent sure that Lil Man was lurking nearby. I had to grab another crib over on 83rd and Phillips. It was low-key enough. JoJo's ass was good and pregnant. At almost six months, she was big as shit. Lil Mama paid a tutor to come by and home-school us both. I needed to take things to another level. I was trying to establish myself, so when it was time to graduate I could jump right into this business management course and open my barber shop. I wanted to be a real estate agent; but since my ace boon-coon died, I wanted to open a hair shop in her memory.

"What'chu up in here doing?"

"Thinking, Biggie Smalls. You hungry?"

"I'm always hungry."

"Alright. I'm 'bout to cook."

I had been taking care of JoJo. I was really starting to care for her. She had some family support, but lately her cousin and auntie ain't been fucking with her. I could tell it bothered her. My friendship with Re was really suffering. She won't even come in when her and JuJu come through. I wasn't about to kick JoJo out for her because she was a damn retard.

"Damn, E, somebody keeps playing on my phone."

"Change your number then."

"I did already."

"Well, do it again or you gon' keep having problems."

(Knock, Knock)

I jumped up; and before I could reach for my gun, JoJo was handing it to me.

"Go in the back, JoJo."

When she was safely in the back, I opened the door. It was Meech.

"What the hell you doing this way?"

"Dirty Man, I need to holla at you."

"Come in."

I wondered what was so important that he couldn't say over the phone.

"How's the arm?"

"I'm good. My trigger finger works better than ever. What brings you this way?"

"I need to holla at JoJo."

"Why?"

"Are you still in touch with her?"

I was skeptical about that question. Before I could say yes or no, she walked up on us. Young's eyes damn near popped out of his head."

"Damn, Joe, you big as shit, girl."

"What you wanna talk to me for, Meech?"

"What's the deal with your cousin, Spooky?"

JoJo's eyes grew big as hell.

"How do you know she's my cousin?"

"She's messing with Money Man. I need to know if she ever said anything about us that we need to be aware of?"

"All she said was that she was on a mission to find out who killed her father. When she does, she said that Carmen was going to help her handle her business."

I was confused like shit. Meech saw my facial expression.

"I'll tell you the whole story later. Where does she live?"

"She be at our auntie's other crib on 79th and Essex."

"I need you to help me get at Lil Man."

"Meech, I'm six months pregnant. What can I do?"

"He'll never bother you again. I promise, I won't miss. I need to get him."

She thought about it for a few seconds.

"Alright, I'll help you. I got a plan that will make him come out of hiding. It's gonna take a few minutes. Let me have my baby. Can you wait?"

"I ain't got no choice."

Lil Man

"WHERE THE FUCK IS SHE?"

I had been posted across the street from Dirty's crib for almost two months. There ain't been no sign of either one of them bitches. I can't believe I lost her.

(Ring, Ring)

I didn't feel like being bothered. I picked up the phone without even looking at the caller I.D.

"What!"

"Uh uh, mothafucker. Don't answer the phone like that. Where the fuck have you been?"

"Looking for your punk ass sister. She ain't staying with Dirty no more."

"Come on 9th and Essex. I'm at my auntie's crib. I got somebody over here that knows where JoJo at."

"I'll call you when I'm outside

I pulled off in my latest stolen car heading to a destination that I really didn't want to be at. Mia was something that I didn't feel like doing. I was tired of all this conniving shit. That bitch was pitiful. She wasn't really 'bout that life. If she was, she'd just kill everybody she had a problem with instead of playing with them. I called her when I hit 18th and Essex and told her to come outside. She makes me wanna stick nails in her eyes. That's how annoying she was.

"Hey lil' bruh?"

"Whud up? Who you got with you that could lead me to JoJo?"

I wasted no time getting down to business.

"My cousin."

No sooner than she said that, this chick came out of the door. My palms started sweating. I knew that face. I started giggling to keep from snapping. That bitch shot and killed my cousin, BayBay when we rushed that spot in Englewood.

"Lil Man, this is my cousin, Spooky."

She smiled like she didn't have a care in the world.

"So, you JoJo's baby daddy? I know where she at. I also got her new number if you want it."

TWENTY-EIGHT

Lil Mama

It had been almost three months since I found out that shit about Carmen. The night Ashley invited us out to talk and squash the beef, I declined. There was no way that I wasn't going to show my ass. I would have ruined the whole plan because I would have shot that sneaky bitch. She's been really feeling herself lately too She was still doing the same disappearing acts on the weekend. I didn't even care anymore because I turned my feelings off. I just wanted to bust her ass out. She was on a countdown to die anyway.

Ring Ring

I looked at my phone and saw that it was Ashley. What the fuck did she want? I didn't bother telling her that we were fucking the same bitch.

"Well hello stranger. What?"

"I would like to know why you are texting my girl asking her why the fuck she's not answering her phone?"

"Huh?" I was actually shocked. "Yo girl? Who Carmen?"

"Yes, my girl."

"Well, I've been fucking our girl for over four months. I doubt if she was your girl back then."

I heard nothing.

"Thought so."

"That little grey-eyed bitch!"

"How you find out it was me texting her? I'm not saved in her phone under Lil Mama."

"Boo told me after I called her when I found the text."

"BOO?"

"She also told me that we needed to squash this bullshit between us."

"You're the one in your feelings, Ashley. I'm cool."

"I'm good now. I forgive you. You mad about Cee? I'm not."

"I'm Gucci," I lied. I was in my feelings. Nigga's and bitches ain't shit. "So how you wanna bust this hoe out, Ash?"

"She's on her way over here right now. Come through."

I jumped up and grabbed my Air Max's and headed for the door.

"I'm on my way."

"Leave your gun at home."

After I fucked Carmen's ass up, I was going to curse Boo's ass out for talking about me with that bitch!

Carmen

"Ashley, I'm on my way. You want something before I get there?"

"Nope, just come on."

Click

What the hell was her problem? I hope it wasn't that time of the month. I wanted some pussy. For the last few days, she's been acting funny. And if that wasn't enough, Lil Mama been ice cold. I think it's time that I find me some more pussy.

Ring, Ring

Speaking of the devil. It was Lil Mama.

"What's good baby?"

"Shit, where you at?"

"On my way to drop some money off to Spooky."

"Oh yeah? Well, come see me when you done."

"Alright."

I don't know what crawled up Lil Mama's ass, but she can kick rocks with that attitude. I pulled up to Ashley's crib and smiled when I saw her waiting for me on the porch. Damn, she must be thirsty for some of this long stroke.

"Hey sexy, why you waiting for me out here. It's cold as shit, girl."

"I just wanted to see you that bad. Come on in here. I got a surprise for you."

I hoped it was another bitch. I liked treats. When I walked in the house, I could feel all the color drain from my face.

Lil Mama

After I called Cee to see where she was, I was furious. I made it to Ashley's house in record time. I pulled my car in the garage and made my way into the house. My stomach started to flip. I smelled a very familiar scent. Cee smelled like this when she came to my home. Ashley saw the look on my face and laughed.

"Bitch, don't start tripping. Why you looking like that?"

"When she comes to my house, I smell this scent on her."

"Well, when she comes over here, I smell . . ."

"Marc Jacob Dot. I finished her sentence, because that's the perfume that I've been wearing.

"Here she comes, Lil Mama . . . hide."

"Bitch I'm not hiding shit."

I sat on her leather couch and folded my legs. I was about to put these hands and feet on this bitch. When she finally walked in, her face dropped.

"Surprise, bitch!"

Carmen

"Surprise bitch!"

I was stuck on stupid, I swear. My face showed it all. Think! Man, I got this shit under control. I was a player.

"What's good, Lil Mama?"

I sat down across from her. I was so nervous that I smiled, trying to lighten up the mood. Why did I do that?

"Oh, you think it's funny?"

I tried to move out of the way, but I wasn't quick enough.

WHAM

She hit me so hard that I saw stars. I jumped up trying to recover, but she caught me in my eye with two more jabs. And what made matters worse, she started talking shit to me while she was fucking me up.

"You gon' try and shit on me like that, bitch? This my city, pussy-ass bitch."

"Ashley, get this crazy-ass bitch off me."

"Hell naw! Fuck you. Punch her ass for me too, Lil Mama."

I slept on this girl for real. Man, she fights like a nigga. I had to get the fuck out of this house. I got my chance when she slipped on the throw rug. I pushed her down and took off running out the door. I was almost at my car when I heard Ashley scream.

"LIL MAMA . . . NOOOO!"

BOC!, BOC!

Two bullets whizzed by my head missing me by an inch.

"Bitch, quit playing."

"Do I look like I'm playing? Yo days are numbered, bitch!"

Damn, I thought I knew her. She had me fucked up if she thought I was going to let this shit ride. My eye was swollen. Yeah, I was coming back for that hoe!

TWENTY-NINE

Mia

I fucked up big time. I had him, gah damn it . . . I had him. Why the fuck didn't I jus' leave him in the basement? Thank goodness I had that trap door put in the pantry. Them little mothafuckers were trying to kill me. I missed my boo though. What we had was real. What? You don't think so? Well I don't give a fuck what you think. He didn't call them to come get him, and the only reason why he left was because they burned the house down. When I called my auntie Cee and told her what happened, she let me lay low at her spot over east. I wasn't about to let JoJo influence Spooky or Cee's mind. I told them that she played a part in Boogie, Jr., and Ramone's deaths. I had to put my spin on a few things to make it believable. I wasn't finished though. I had a few tricks up my sleeve. All in due time though. I had to reach out to Jaw and let him know that I was okay. I know he probably worried about me. Where the hell is my phone?

"Yo, who's this calling me private?"

"Hey baby, I just wanted to let you know that I was okay. I know you been worried about me."

He was quiet.

"Jaw, did you hear me?"

"You crazy as hell, man. Quit the bullshit."

"I'm pregnant."

I didn't even mean to say that. It just slipped out. I really didn't know if I was or not. I ain't even bothered to take a test. Maybe I needed to.

"You what? Man, that shit ain't funny."

"I'm having our baby and I suggest you get your shit together so we can be a family."

"Man, don't call me private no more. I'ma hit you back later."

I had to hang up and slow my heart rate down. I could get him if I played my cards right.

"Spooky? Come on, let's go to Planned Parenthood. I need to get tested."

JuJu

I had been in a shitty mood all week. Having Jaw back on a consistent basis was annoying. He was trying his best to make me feel better about that whole Mia situation. I just wasn't going for the dumb shit. I still ain't gave him none either. I didn't know what was going on with his beef cake.

"JuJu, we need to talk,"

"If you wanna fuck, the answer is no. You gotta go get checked before I give you anything."

He had the nerve to look at me like I insulted him.

"Why the fuck you looking at me like that, Jaw?"

My blood was boiling now.

"You got me fucked up if you think I'm 'bout to sweat you for some ass. That ain't even what I wanted to holla at you about."

Damn he told me.

"Well, what then?"

"Mia just called me."

"And?"

"She said she pregnant."

That's it! I was holding this shit in for too long. Jaw never saw it coming.

BAM!

I hit him square in his fucking mouth. He stumbled back and looked at me like he wanted to kill me. I wasn't done though.

"I FUCKING HATE YOU!"

I rushed him and swung with all my might. (WHAM!) That punch landed to the side of his head.

"Man, Joe"

BOOM

He picked me up and slammed me on my back. I was appalled.

"Hit me again, Ju. I'ma stomp the shit out of you, I swear to God!"

"GET OUT! I was beyond hurt. I wasn't about to compete with no baby. Fuck waiting for that hoe to find us. I was going to find her. I picked up the phone and called Dirty.

"Hey bald-head scallywag."

"Where JoJo?"

She sensed the aggression in my tone.

"What's wrong?"

"I just jumped on Jaw because he told me that Mia bitch called him saying she was pregnant."

"Daammmmnn!"

"I need JoJo to help me find her."

"Come through. She about to go get some vitamins and shit from Planned Parenthood. You can take her."

I grabbed my keys and headed for the door.

JoJo

10 minutes later

"Damn, E, could you go with me? I don't feel all that comfortable being around your friends."

"Ju, cool. She wanna talk to you about Mia,"

"I don't have shit to say about that hoe."

"I'll let her tell you what's going on."

Knock, Knock

I went to open the door, and when I did I almost slammed it back once. I saw Re standing there. She stuck her foot in the door so it wouldn't slam.

"Bitch!"

"I know. I'ma bad bitch."

"You gon' be a dead bitch if you slam my foot in the door again."

E quickly came out of the room with her shit on.

"Come on, Re, let's roll."

"You better get that . . ."

"Come on, Re, damn."

She looked at me and stuck up her middle finger.

"I love you too, Re."

As soon as they left, JuJu called me.

"I'm downstairs, JoJo."

I hoped this went well. I was tired of the bullshit.

THIRTY

Young Meech

❝❝So nigga, what's the plan? It's been long enough. I want Lil Man's ass."

"Call Money Man. Ole girl like seven and a half months pregnant. We gotta wait like six more weeks. We gon' use that baby to bring that nigga out."

"The baby? Maw, I don't care who's baby it is. I'm not with that."

"It's gonna work, and the baby ain't gon' get hurt. Trust me."

I hope that was the case. I just wanted to end all of this madness. I couldn't go on with my life unless that nigga was dead. I didn't care about nothing else at this point. Money Man and Outlaw were some true hustlers. They knew what I was going through, so they picked up my slack. When I slept at night, my dreams haunted me. I saw visions of Tyesha, Tiki, and my Auntie Shawn. I wake up crying because I feel like I let them down. That's a fucked-up feeling to have.

"Money Man, what's up with ya girl? I ain't seen her around."

"She still doing what I need her to do as far as the work side, but, man, shorty the enemy. I'ma get her ass. She's playing a dangerous game."

"JoJo said that she hanging with that bitch, Mia, so you know she's tainted more now than ever."

"She knows too much. It's time for her to die."

"They're all going to die."

Lil Mama

"Bitch, you get on my nerves. I told you not to act a fool yet. I bet she know that we know who she really is."

"No she don't! That ass-whooping was personal."

"You shot at her, too."

"You and Ashley besties or something?"

"No, but she'll tell me what you won't."

"Speaking of telling, why did you feel the need to tell her that I was the one texting Cee?"

"Because I wanted to bitch. You wasn't."

"What the fuck ever. I think we should just go whack that hoe and steal all her work and be done with it."

"I'm with it. I'm calling Heidi. Meet me at Shawn's crib. We gon' need some extra help if we gon' rob the hoe, too."

"I'll be there."

I hadn't heard from that no-good ass bitch since I put these paws on her. I hated a sneaky-ass mothafucker. I grabbed my gun and my purse and headed for the door. Aww shit, I forgot to turn off my space heater. Fuck around and burn my lil' crib down. As soon as I opened my front door . . *CRACK!*, I fell flat on my ass.

"Going somewhere?"

"You had to snake me?"

"Shut up bitch."

WHAM!

My head hit the ground hard as fuck. I knew that I was I trouble. She grabbed me by my hair and drug me back into my apartment. I couldn't let this hoe isolate me in this house. If I did, I was a dead bitch.

Boo

I hope that this was the last time we had to murder anybody. This ain't even 'bout getting money no more. This world is too damn small, and Big Moe's family is damn sure too big. I picked Heidi up first so I could let her know what we were about to do.

When she got in the car, I was surprised. She was dressed appropriately for the occasion. She slammed my door when she got in the car.

"Bitch. what the hell?"

"You don't respect our friendship."

"Huh? What are you talking about?"

"I told you that I wasn't on all this 007 shit, but yet you keep coming to get me."

"If that's how you feel then Heidi, you don't have to come."

"So what? Let you go by yourself? Hell no, because if you die, yo ass is gonna haunt me for the rest of my life. You know I don't do ghosts. Let's do this, but after this, I mean it, no more killing!"

"I hope after this we won't have to."

Lil Mama hadn't hit me back to let me know that she made it to Shawn's spot. Heidi knew my facial expressions so well.

"What now?"

"Lil Mama ain't called me back yet."

"I'm sick of that bony-ass hoe. Hit her house first then."

Twenty minutes later, I was pulling across the street from Lil Mama's house. Her car was still outside, and she wasn't answering her phone.

"A'ight, Heidi, something ain't right. She ain't answering her phone and her car right there," I pointed.

"Boo, call the police."

"The police? Why?"

"I got a bad feeling about this one. My stomach is in knots, and no I don't have to shit. Something just ain't right."

"Well, we're about to find out. I'm not calling no fucking police."

"Okay then, call Ashley at least."

I should call her. I dialed her number.

"Hey chick!"

"Long story short, Lil Mama might be in trouble. I need you. Meet me at her crib."

"I'm on my way."

"There, she's on the way. Ready?"

We went around the back because she had a big-ass window in her living room overlooking the street. Creeping up the back stairwell was not an easy task. The stairs creaked. Heidi was taking them two at a time.

"Come on here, Boo. The more you try not to make noise, the more noise you gon' make."

When we made it to the top of the stairs, I heard Lil Mama scream.

"Arrrggghhhh!"

Oh my God. She was in trouble. Heidi kicked the door in and started shooting.

BOC!, BOC!, BOC!

THIRTY-ONE

JuJu

I didn't know what to do. I loved Jaw, but I just couldn't accept no baby, especially not from that crazy-ass bitch, Mia. When I picked up JoJo, I almost felt uncomfortable talking about her sister. I guess she sensed my apprehensiveness.

"Ju, what you wanna talk about? E said you wanted to get at Mia. I don't blame you. She needs to be stopped."

"She called Jaw and said she was pregnant."

JoJo started cracking up. I didn't find that shit funny at all. I was about to put her fat-ass out.

"Damn, JoJo, my feelings are hurt. Stop fucking laughing."

"I'm sorry, JuJu. That bitch is pitiful. Look, she can't have kids."

"Really? What chu talking 'bout, JoJo?"

"She got pregnant with her first boyfriend's baby, and when she killed him, she aborted the baby. Well they must have done something wrong because she had to be rushed to the hospital. They ended up taking her uterus out."

That was all I needed to hear. I instantly perked up.

"Girl, you don't know you just saved Jaw's life."

We started laughing as I pulled into the Planned Parenthood parking lot.

"Aww, shit!"

"What, JoJo?"

She pointed. "There goes Mia and Spooky right there."

"Aww, hell yeah. I'm 'bout to beat that hoe's ass."

Dirty E

"I was tired of dealing with Re's unstable ass. She was one of my best friends, but that didn't excuse her behavior."

"Re, man, you need to . . . ."

"Don't tell me what I need to do. You choosing that hoe over me?"

"Are we fucking?"

"WHAT?"

"You starting to sound like my bitch."

WHACK!

"Aww bitch!"

That crazy bitch hit me in the shoulder I got shot in.

"Re, what the hell, man?"

"Don't talk to me like that. You know I'm sensitive."

"I was about to punch her punk-ass back when my phone rang. It was JoJo.

"Whud up, fat girl?"

Re rolled her eyes at me and smacked her lips. Drama Queen.

"You need to get up here at the Planned Parenthood on 1100 and Division."

"What's going on?"

"When we pulled into the parking lot, we saw Mia. Now JuJu 'bout to fight her. My cousin, Spooky, tryin' to jump."

"We on our way. JoJo, whatever you do, don't let her get jumped."

"E, I'm pregnant. What . . ."

"I DON'T GIVE A FUCK! DON'T LET THEM JUMP HER!"

I hung up.

"Re, get to 1100 South Division ASAP!"

Mia

"Girl, yo ass crazy."

I couldn't believe how funny Spooky was.

"Money Man thinks I'm so innocent. I really wanna fuck Young Meech. He's the boss."

I guess she really didn't know whose son he was.

"Yeah, he's a boss just like his father was."

"Was? Who was his father?"

"King Meech. Your father's best friend until he started fucking King's baby mother."

"What? Wait, my daddy was fucking his best friend's girl?"

"Yep and he had King killed too."

I knew I had her ass now.

"Who killed King?"

"Ramone."

"Does Young know this?"

"Of course he knows. That's why he killed Uncle T and his own mother."

I told her the story that was told to me by my auntie's girlfriend.

"Don't trip, Spooky. We gon' get everyone responsible for our unhappiness."

I pulled in the parking lot and gave her a hug.

"We gotta stick together. It's a cold world out here."

As we were exiting my car, I locked eyes with the one bitch that was standing in the way of my happiness.

"Spooky, look. There go them bitches, JuJu and JoJo. You ready to get down?"

"Aw yeah. You know I can throw these thangs."

I did underestimate the small girl's quickness. As soon as I stepped out of the car all hell broke loose.

JuJu

BAM!

I wasted no time getting my issue off my chest.

"Talk that lil' girl shit now."

BAM!

I punched her dead in her eye.

"You pregnant?"

KICK

"Not after today."

I kicked her square in her stomach. She wasn't fucking with me. I was on beast mode. She was on the ground trying to use the car as leverage to stand up.

WHACK!

I slammed her head into the car door.

"You got . . . *WHACK!* . . . me . . . *BAM!* . . . fucked *CRACK!*. . . up."

She was on the verge of passing out. I was about to Mortal Combat finish her ass until this bitch caught me off guard and snuck me from my blind side.

BAM!

Spooky

I was ready. Mia had just dropped some news on me that I wasn't expecting. T was in the company of the enemy the whole time. As soon as Mia got out of the car, ole girl dropped her.

"Damn!"

I got out of the car and let them get head up. Well I thought it was going to be a good fight especially after all that rah-rah shit Mia was talking. But from the looks of it, whoever that bitch was, she was whooping Mia's ass. I had seen enough. If I didn't help her, Mia's ass was about to be knocked out. Ole girl never saw me coming

BAM!

She staggered back a bit. She looked at me with that 'you know you done fucked up' look.

"Oh yeah! You want some, too?"

I was ready, or so I thought. She came at me like a skilled boxer. She was bouncing around and shit. I was trying to watch her hands. Wrong move!

WHACK!, WHACK!

She hit me so fast I got stuck. I bounced back though. I'm far from a punk.

"Let's dance hoe."

BOP, BOP

I gave her a nice two-piece combo before she stuck me again. I saw Mia getting up, so I knew she was about to jump in. I saw Mia pick up a bottle. She was about to hit ole girl with it, when all of a sudden, JoJo's fat ass came out of nowhere.

JoJo

I didn't even have time to talk JuJu's ass out of fighting. She jumped out of the car and got on Mia's ass. I was speechless. That girl was on a mission. Ain't never seen my sister get her ass served like that. JuJu was wearing that ass out. Gaahhh damn! I sat there watching not knowing what to do. I thought I was in the clear until Spooky snuck JuJu.

"Fuck!"

I jumped out of the car and joined the party. Mia was shaking off the ass-whooping Ju put on her. JuJu was tapping Spooky's ass. Damn, that bitch had wings as if she drank a Red Bull. I stood there until I saw Mia charge at JuJu with a bottle. She was so hell-bent on hitting her that she never saw me.

WHAM

"Uh, bitch!"

She dropped the bottle and looked at me.

"Bitch, I'm 'bout to beat that baby out of you."

I got ready to fight to the death because I was going to die protecting my baby. I had to. I didn't say shit. We locked like two pit bulls. I didn't have to worry about Spooky because JuJu was literally stomping her head into the ground as if she was a footwork rig in a dance contest. Mia and I went blow for blow until she hit me in my eye causing me to fall backwards. Then the dirty bitch kicked me in my stomach, knocking all the fight I had out of me.

"AARRGGGHHH!"

THIRTY-TWO

Lil Mama

When I came to, Cee had me tied to one of my dining room chairs. She was sitting directly in front of me.

"Welcome back, bitch."

"Wow, that was a nice thing to say to me after you cheated on me."

She stood up and walked up on me. I didn't expect what happened next. She hocked and spit in my face.

"Aww hell, naw bitch, you done lost yo mind. Untie me. You wanna fight?"

"You think I got you tied to a chair because I'm mad about a fight?"

"It wasn't no fight. I hit you and you hit the ground."

"You got a smart-ass mouth. I'ma shoot you in the face like them niggas you was with who shot my brother."

Aww shit! How the fuck did she find out I had something to do with that? I couldn't hide the shock that was plastered on my face. She knew she had me.

"Yeah you quiet now. Talk!"

SMACK

No this bitch didn't just hit me.

"Who told you I had something to do with that?"

"You would rather ask a question than deny the accusation?"

"Deny it for what? I know I'm about to die. I'm cool with that. I just wanna know who told you."

"I'll let you see her face before you take your last breath."

I closed my eyes and said a small prayer.

Knock, Knock

I knew Boo would come once she realized I didn't call her back. Cee opened the door and I braced-myself preparing for the blood splatter and the loud boom that I knew was coming.

"Just in time, baby. Come in."

Huh? That ain't Boo. When I opened my eyes, I swear I peed a little.

"Well Lil Mama. Looks like you in a fucked-up situation. You should call 911. Aww wait, that's me."

"Ashley, what the fuck are you doing?"

"I'm doing what my woman wants me to do. I would help you out, but you let that fat bastard kidnap me. Not only did he kidnap me, but he raped me over and over again. He made me sit in my own shit and piss. Payback is a bitch."

Oh my god, I couldn't believe this funky-ass hoe.

"You told Cee about Big T?"

"Of course I did. Don't worry, I told her that you didn't actually kill him. Poohman did. So instead of trying to kill all of ya'll, I'ma make sure that you die and the rest of them do life in prison: Jaw, Young Meech, Poohman, and Boo."

"Boo wasn't even there."

"Her and Heidi killed A and Blake."

"You fucking bitch."

"I know, thank you. You can die. We don't need you anymore. But before you go, I want you to experience some pain. Cee, go turn on the stove and bring me back something hot."

Cee kissed Ashley and did as she was told.

"Tiki is probably turning over in her grave right now."

"Fuck that lying little bitch. It's because of her that I met ya'll nothing-ass bitches."

Cee came back in the room smiling. She handed Ashley my hot comb. It was red hot. Oh God!

"Open her legs and hold them. I'm going to burn your thighs like he did me and then I'm going to fuck you with this hot comb."

"Bitch, you better kill me."

"Oh, I plan to. Nice and slow."

She pressed the hot comb on my thigh.

"ARRRGGHHHHHHH!"

Heidi

Once I heard her scream, I knew that she needed us. T kicked the door open and starting bussing.

BOC! BOC! BOC!

Me and Boo rushed the crib like the ATF Boys. We almost knocked each other over trying to stop, once we made it to the dining room and saw who was holding a hot comb.

"Ashley, what the fuck are you doing?"

"Getting my revenge."

"Aww, Boo, see I told you that you should have let me knock that bitch out a long time ago. Bitch, why you tryin to burn her leg. You need to get them naps on the back of your neck ya ole nappy-headed bitch!"

Boo

I couldn't believe my eyes either.

"Ashley, what the fuck are you doing?"

"Quit asking me that shit. What the fuck does it look like?"

Click, Clack

I cocked my gun. I wasn't about to play with her.

"Sis, you good?"

"Man, Joe, shoot this bitch."

"And you," I pointed to Gee, "are going to die too, bitch."

I looked at Heidi to see if she was ready. To my surprise, she was in killer mode. Never seen that look before. Somebody was about to die.

"Fuck all this talking."

POP!, POP!

I let off two rounds. Ashley and Gee scattered.

"Heidi, get Lil Mama."

I dropped low and went looking for they ass. It was dark as hell. I couldn't see shit.

"Are you ready to die?"

Fuck me! Ashley crept up on me and pushed her pistol against my head.

Lil Man

"Heidi, you gotta shoot that bitch! My leg is burned really badly. Ain't no running. Go get her!"

I crawled under the dining room table and called for reinforcements.

"Yo, what up?"

"Get to my crib now! We in trouble."

I hoped that help came in time.

THIRTY-THREE

ReRe

""Pull over right there, Re."

"I am."

When we pulled up, those hoes were out there brawling. JuJu was stomping some girl and JoJo's ass was banging it out with her sister. When she fucked up and slipped, ole' girl kicked her in the stomach. She dropped to the ground and screamed. Dirty snapped.

"JOJO!"

She jumped out of the car, pistol in hand.

"E, NO!"

Mia never saw it coming.

BOC!, BOC!, BOC!, BOC!, BOC!

Damn, she emptied the whole clip in that girl. Mia dropped like a ton of bricks. JuJu ran to help pick up JoJo.

"Oh god. My water just broke!"

"E, we gotta go before the police come."

When I saw E bring that hoe to my car, I hit my locks.

"Uh-uh. That bitch ain't getting in here."

The look E game me sent a clear message that maybe our friendship was over. Ju handed E the keys to her car and got in the car with me. The girl she crawled over to Mia and started screaming. Oh shit, it was time to go. Ju looked at me and shook her head.

"You really need to quit. Follow Dirty to the hospital."

"I'm not!"

"FOLLOW HER!"

Damn, why the fuck is everybody so mad at me? I'm only looking out for them. JoJo was the enemy. She was about to have the enemy's baby. Why be mad at me?

Dirty E

"OH, GOD. E, GET ME TO THE HOSPITAL!"

"Be cool, shorty, we almost there!"

"It hurts so bad."

I hit the expressway flying like a bat out of hell. Re made me wanna shoot her ol' evil ass. I made it to Rush in no time.

"I think the head is coming out. OH GOD!"

I stuck my hand between her legs and I'll be damned! The head was crowning. I jumped out of the car and ran in the emergency room door to find a doctor. I was freaking out!

"S-s-somebody help me, please. My friend is having her baby!""

Two nurses ran outside with a stretcher. Two seconds later, they came back with a screaming JoJo.

"IT HURTS! TAKE IT OUT!"

I ran back outside to park my car. Ju and ReRe were walking up as I parked. I didn't have shit to say to Re's ass. They followed me without saying a word.

JoJo

Labor pains ain't no joke. I swear the shit hurt like hell. I didn't even get a chance to get pain medicine. My little girl was almost out.

"Push, baby, push. You almost done. One more big push. There!"

Out came my little girl. She came out hollering, which was a good sign. I was exhausted. I thanked God that when I opened my eyes, E was there with the nurses making sure everything was good. The nurse came and brought me my baby. E was smiling like a proud father.

"JoJo, you sure that baby ain't mine?"

The nurse looked at her and shook her head.

"She's kidding."

"She's small but very healthy overall. Would you like to hold her?"

When she gave me my baby, the first thing I noticed were those signature hazel eyes.

"Damn you are a cute little girl. Yes you are."

She looked at me and smiled. I didn't see any resemblance to Derrick. Thank God.

Knock, Knock

In came JuJu and Re. Oh Lord.

"Aww JoJo, let me see her."

JuJu held her and sat next to me.

"She is so cute. Hey pretty mama."

The creepiest thing happened. She started giggling as if JuJu said the funniest thing in the world. Me and JuJu locked eyes. I hope she would be nothing like him. Re walked out of the room.

Spooky

"Ma'am, can you tell me who did this?"

I didn't say shit. I just listened to the EMTs talk.

"Shit, she's lucky to be alive. Whoever beat her ass meant business.

"Well, at least she didn't end up like that other one."

"Once we get to Rush, we'll let the doctor's know she's a minor. Do you want us to call anybody for you?"

I didn't have shit to say. Wait until I run into the hoes again. It was going to be on!

"We're here."

ReRe

I didn't know what to feel. I knew that my besties love me. I just wondered how they could forgive her for that shit she took part in. When I saw JuJu happily holding Lil Man's baby, it made me sick. I walked out of the room to call Poohman. He wasn't answering the phone. Shit! I wanted to hurt somebody, bad.

"Clear the way."

I moved out of the way so the paramedics could wheel in somebody. When I turned around, I almost did a happy dance. It was the bitch JuJu beat up. I played it cool. I saw them roll her into exam room four. I walked back toward the maternity ward. I needed some scrubs. After I found what I was looking for, I made my way to exam room four.

Machine beeping

Damn. JuJu beat her ass bad. Her eyes were closed shut. This bitch looked like leap frog. I looked around the room for something I could use as a weapon. I found a syringe. I heard that if you pumped air into an I.V., the air bubble would travel to your heart and kill you Well, let's see! I unplugged the machines so the alarms wouldn't alert the nurse. Once I pushed the air into the I.V., her eyes popped open as much as they could. I slapped my hand on her face and held her down. She didn't have much fight left in her. Ole punk-ass bitch. After I checked her pulse to make sure she was dead, I used a napkin to wipe off everything I touched. Dang, I feel so much better. Rest in hell, bitch!

THIRTY-FOUR

Heidi

"Stay put, Lil Mama, I'm about to find Boo. Where the fuck is the light switch? It's dark as fuck."

This is some crazy-ass Law and Order-type shit. It's always some drama with us. I need some new friends. Never in a million years did I ever think that Boo would get me in so much bullshit. Okay, okay, it ain't all her fault. I was all for the bullshit in the beginning, but shit got real and people started dying. The streets ain't no joke. It was dark as shit in this hoe. Let me find out Lil Mama didn't pay her light bill. I hit the corner and instantly saw stars.

BAM!

"Who the fuck hit me?"

That bitch, Cee, laughed and punched me in my stomach. That shit made me fart and knocked the wind out of me.

"OUCH!"

Down to my knees I went. I guess this was it. Didn't look like we were going to be saved today. I looked at Boo and it broke my heart. This was the last time I was going to see my girl. She looked at me.

"I love you, Heidi."

"Bitch, I'ma kill you for getting me killed."

I closed my eyes for what I thought would be forever. Ashley laughed at me.

"Cee, shoot that bitch!"

BOC!, BOC!

I screamed when I felt Boo's blood splash on my face.

Jaw

BOC!, BOC!

My mama screamed, scaring the shit out of me.

"Bitch, put that gun down."

I couldn't believe my eyes. Ashley was holding a gun to my Auntie Boo's head.

"What the fuck is going on?"

My mama jumped up and went to grab Boo, but Ashley pulled her back and held her tight, pressing her gun to her temple.

"That dirty bitch was fucking T's sister."

Damn!

"Fuck you. Lil Mama was fucking her, too. You killed my boo. I'm walking out of here. Ya'll ain't dumb enough to kill a cop."

POP! POP! POP!

Boo dropped to the ground and my mama went to grab her thinking she was shot.

"BOO!"

My mother went crazy. Boo sat up and wiped the blood off of her face.

"I'm fine bitch, move. Who the fuck shot her?"

"I did."

Poohman came walking out of the shadows.

"Nigga, yo aim on point boy. How you manage that?"

"Ask Boo."

"Thank God Lil Mama's freaky-ass likes mirrors. I saw Poohman creeping through the kitchen because of that mirror on the mantle. Why the fuck did you think I was leaning to the side?"

"Shit, I don't know, auntie, I thought you were trying to make a run for it."

"Who called ya'll?"

"I did."

Lil Mama came limping into the room. Her leg was fucked up.

"I'm good. Just get me to the hospital."

How were we going to explain this shit to the police?

"Lil Mama, the police . . ."

"The camera on the mantle will explain."

THIRTY-FIVE

Young Meech

Two weeks later

I was furious that my mom was almost killed. Jaw and Poohman saved the day. I was beyond grateful. I didn't have time to be sad. Today was the happiest day of my life. JoJo was out of the hospital and she agreed to help me get Lil Man. We didn't have to worry about Mia and Money Man's bitch. Dirty and Re did that. We got a killa squad that ain't to be fucked with.

I was on my way to get JoJo when my phone rang. It was JoJo. I hoped she wasn't calling to change her mind.

"Young, when you get here, I need to go to K-Mart."

"Come outside."

JoJo

The last two weeks were the best two weeks of my life. My daughter is so precious. I named her Tyshawn Christina. E was in love with her and them hazel eyes. It was still uncomfortable to speak about her father, so I didn't. I had been planning to help Meech get Derrick, so I've been in touch with him. He wanted to see her so badly. I just knew that the day I let him see her would be the last day of my life. The plan was for me to tell him to meet me so he could see the baby. Meech was going to shoot him and then we'd live happily ever after. For some reason, I knew that it wouldn't end like that. If all went well, I'd finally be done with him for good. Everybody loved her except ReRe. She didn't even come around. E was supposed to be here by now. I wanted to take care of this shit and get back to my baby. Derrick was going to be surprised when he shows up and there's no baby. I hit E and JuJu's phone . . . nothing. I decided to try Re's phone.

"Hello?"

"Re, this JoJo. Is E over there?"

"No, and don't call me, bitch. We ain't cool."

CLICK

I called Meech. I had an idea.

"Come outside."

When I got in the car I told him to take me to Re's house because E was there. The whole ride over I felt like this was a bad idea. When we pulled up, I grabbed my baby's car seat and the baby bag. After that, I told Young to take me to K-Mart.

"You think this is gon' work?"

"I hope so. Let me call him to see where he's at."

Lil Man

"Where you at?"

"Meet me at the lakefront on 19th. The one by Rainbow Beach."

"Bye."

I knew she was bringing somebody with her. I was ready though. If she was all about that peace shit she been talking, then why not meet me where you live? I mean it's still too cold to bring my baby outside. I was onto her ass. I hoped she give me my baby without any problems.

Young Meech

"I'ma drop you and the car seat off right here. You gon'
have to walk through the park.

"You strapped?"

"Yeah, Meech. I'm scared."

"I can't tell you that everything is going to be okay
because you know what type of person we dealing with.
Just get ready and duck."

"I just want her to be safe."

"If anything happens to you, God forbid I got her."

"Okay, let's do this."

JoJo

I had Young drop me off two blocks away from the
park. I walked the rest of the way in case he was watching.
My phone rang. It was him.

"Sit at the bench in front of you."

"Where you at, Derrick?"

"Walking towards you."

Sure enough, when I sat down he was walking toward
me with a smile on his face.

"What's good, baby mama?"

"Hey Derrick."

"Why'd you cross me, JoJo? I had your back no matter how bad you thought I treated you."

"You were bogus and reckless. If I wanted this baby to have a normal life, I had to leave you."

He smiled, which made me shiver.

"You didn't have to try and get me killed."

"I didn't . . ."

"BITCH, DON'T LIE TO ME!"

"Stop yelling before you wake her up."

Lord, Meech! Where are you?

Young Meech

I had a clean shot. My heart was racing. My hands were shaking. I needed to calm down before I pulled the trigger. I saw Lil Man getting animated.

"Keep him calm, JoJo."

I was finally able to focus. The rifle I had come with a scope, so I had a clean and clear shot. All I had to do was pull the trigger.

"Die nigga."

I pulled the trigger.

Lil Man

This bitch thought I was stupid. I knew she wasn't alone. I was done playing with her.

"Let me see my baby?"

"No, not right here. It's windy outside."

"Well, you should have thought about that before you decided to meet me outside."

When I went to pull the blanket down, I heard something zip past my head and hit tree. I looked at her and smiled.

"He missed."

I pulled out my gun and pulled the trigger.

BOC! BOC! BOC!

She looked surprised when I shot her between her eyes *Giggling*. I grabbed my baby and the bag and walked off.

Young Meech

FUCK, FUCK, FUCK! I missed. I watched in pure terror as he shot JoJo in the head three times. I let go of the last few tears I had in my soul. Her blood was on my hands. I picked up the phone to call Dirty.

"Yo, what?"

"JoJo's dead, Dirty. Lil Man just shot her over here in Rainbow Park on 119th."

E could hear her crying on the other end of the phone. That killed me.

"Where's the baby?"

"Baby? You got her."

"No the fuck I don't, Young."

"I took her to Re's because she said you was there. We left the baby there."

"Oh my God! Please don't let this baby be hurt. Meet me at Re's."

Lil Man

Once I finally made it back to the car, I turned on the heat. I knew my baby was probably cold. I sat the car seat on the passenger seat and pulled down the blanket.

"Hey! Daddy's little . . . what the fuck?"

It was a baby doll strapped in the car seat. There was a note pinned to her chest:

Lil Man – You stupid mothafucker. You took me away from our child. You will never see her! EVER! I knew that you were going to kill me. I'll rest in peace knowing that you will never have her. See you in hell.

JuJu

I couldn't breathe.

"BITCH, WHERE IS MY BABY?"

I bawled like a baby. She was the only thing in the world that would have made me do right. I was going to find her. This shit wasn't over. I had to continue on with my plans without her for now. I knew that the police were going to be looking for me soon. I was going to get the last laugh!

THIRTY-SIX

ReRe

This weed I was smoking was some huff. It had me hallucinating. I swear that I heard a baby crying. I got up off the couch to get me some juice and the crying got louder. It was coming from the front door. I opened the door thinking I was going crazy. What I saw made me drop my glass of juice. What the hell was a baby doing on my door step? I picked up the car seat and closed the door. When I took a good look at the baby, my blood started boiling. Is this some type of joke? I was now staring into the eyes of a baby whose father destroyed my life. He killed my sister, Tiki. I noticed there was a note on the side of her:

Dear ReRe – If you are reading this letter, then that means that I am dead. Please don't let Lil Man get my baby. I tried to fix my wrongs, but he got me. You are probably staring into my baby's eyes with a heart full of hate. If you hate her that much because of who her parents are, then send my baby's soul to me. I'm sorry for the pain I've caused you and your friends. You have my baby's life in your hands. I'll be waiting at heaven's gate for my baby.

I was overwhelmed with so many emotions that I broke down and cried. The baby started to cry as well. I didn't know what to do. I hated this baby because I hated her parents. I cried harder. She cried harder, too. All she wanted was for me to hold her. I didn't have the love in me that she needed. Or did I? As soon as I picked her up, she stopped crying. I cried even harder. If only this baby knew that I never wanted her to exist. I held her close to my chest, and she cooed in my ear. I changed her diaper and rocked her to sleep. I held her so tight, because I wanted her to feel safe in my arms.

"Lord, please give me the strength to love this baby."

Dirty E

"Just get there Ju."

I called everybody. ReRe's ass was unpredictable. She hated Lil Man and JoJo that bad that it was a possibility that she'd hurt that baby. Me, Poohman, Jaw, and JuJu all pulled up at the same time. Poohman was the first one up the stairs. He unlocked the door and turned around to face us.

"Whatever happens, just follow my lead."

When he opened the door, we were all expecting the worse. It seemed like all of us were holding our breaths; and when we saw her and the baby unharmed, we exhaled. She was sitting on the couch with the baby in her arms, caressing her little face and hands. Poohman was the first to speak.

"Re, give me the baby, ma."

She was smiling at the baby; but when she looked at us, she gave us the look of death. I ain't gon' lie, she scared the fuck out of me.

"Really? Do I look like a baby killer?"

I walked up next to Poohman.

"Just give her to me. I'll keep her."

"I'm not giving you shit, E. Quit talking to me like I'm some mental patient."

All of us looked at each other and back at her. Bad move!

"Fuck all of ya'll. She's staying right here with me. That's what her mother wanted."

She kissed Tyshawn on her head and rocked her back to sleep.

EPILOGUE

JuJu

Eventually I quit giving Jaw a hard time. We went to counseling because I needed to get some things off of my chest without using violence. We planned on getting married next year when I turn 18. I finished school and enrolled at CSU. I was trying to get my nursing degree. ReRe and Poohman went through the courts; and with the help of Boo, they got full parental rights over Tyshawn. Re got her diploma, too. She's currently enrolled at Olive Harvey College, majoring in child development. Poohman and Jaw took over Englewood, Roseland, and a few spots out west. They're doing big things, too. Got a few beauty supply stores and they also bought into a McDonald franchise. After E finished school, she opened up her own hair shop. She named it Razor Sharp. She's Tyshawn's god-daddy. She also got her a new girlfriend. Everything turned out for the best, even though we went through hell and hot water to get here.

Boo

After the shootout at Lil Mama's crib, Heidi decided that she didn't wanna be thug any more. These days you can find her at home baking cookies with the grandbabies watching movies. She actually took cooking and baking lessons. The police decided not to charge Poohman and Jaw with the murders of Cee and Officer Dixon. I still can't believe that she let pussy turn her against us. I guess she couldn't let go of the hatred she felt towards Lil Mama. Oh well, the bitch is better off dead. Me and Lil Mama opened a few nightclubs throughout the city. I met a big-time boss nigga. Pussy so good the nigga popped two babies in me. My sons, Armon and Demarion, are my life. Fuck with 'em and the old Boo will show her face. Lil Mama is still single. She said the only thing that she wants to be obligated to is her period every month. That's the only thing she said she was going to keep track of. That hoe crazy! Don't sleep on the Chi! We still out here moving silently through these streets. Remember the loudest mothafucker ain't making no noise!

Young Meech

The Chi City Boys took the low-end by storm. Money Man is still my right hand. Outlaw's crazy ass is still my young shooter. Niggas on the street know what is. After JoJo's death, I fell into a dark hole. Me wanting that nigga that bad caused that baby to lose her mother. I kept my promise. Even though Re got her, I bring her whatever she need and want every week. That's my lil' Fat-Fat.

I could never hate her because of who her father was and what he did to me. That nigga disappeared. Nobody has seen or heard from him. I would say that the nigga tucked his tail and ran; but even though I hate his guts, I gotta give him his props. He ain't that kind of dude, so I know I'ma see his ass again. When I do, it's lights out. I lost a lot but I gained so much more. I finally got me a new girl. She's smart and pretty as hell. She also a beast if I need her to be. Even though I'm still running a drug enterprise, I get tutored every day. I promised Lil Mama I'd finish school. My future looking bright. These streets ain't ready for Young Meech and the Chi City Boys. Me and my crew gon' continued to climb to the top. Any nigga or bitch that get in our way gon' learn the hard way. Ain't no stopping us. And whenever Lil Man ready to show his face, I'ma be ready to blow that ugly mothafucka off!

Lil Man

Yeah, I know ya'll probably wanted me dead by now, but nope. It ain't my time to die yet. I'm not done. You think I'ma let them mothafuckers keep my daughter? Hell fucking no! I'm coming back for what's mine, and I'm killing whoever get in my way. I'ma 'bout to go down South and get my mind right and my weight up. I'm coming back bigger, badder, and better! Go ahead and sleep on Lil Man. I ain't got no problem coming to wake yo ass up!

BOOKS BY GOOD2GO AUTHORS